SAVAGE HIGHWAY

SAVAGE HIGHWAY

Jack Moskovitz

RAMBLE HOUSE

ISBN 13: 978-1-60543-445-2

ISBN 10: 1-60543-445-0

Cover Art: Gavin L. O'Keefe
Preparation: Fender Tucker

To
JOHNNIE MAE,
WHO LOVES GARAGE SALES,
KITTENS AND OLD MEN NAMED JACK.

SAVAGE HIGHWAY

ONE

STEVE JONES DETOURED off I-680 to avoid the weigh station.

The two lane county road through Arnholt, Nebraska was mud slick. Drivers were warned of possible freezing drizzle before dusk.

Ahead, the pickup in the deuce and a half's lane slowed without flashing its warning signal.

Jones tapped the air brakes, tapped the horn. The horn's echo clattered against the tightly grouped vacant store fronts on both sides of the eight lane main street.

The wind picked up.

The corner diner's neon pierced the swirling fog. Jones geared down, eased toward the adjoining lane. The pickup cut into that lane and swerved avoiding the three-ton transport's bumper. Jones slammed his fist against the steering wheel. The horn made a nasal sound.

The shotgun above the windshield visor rattled.

A woman in the pickup's passenger seat turned. She flashed the finger.

Steve reached for the twelve gauge.

The pickup stopped at the curb. The woman pulled a younger woman across the seat, and into the rain.

The younger woman shrieked: "Damn you, no."

"Damn me, yes."

The buxom woman tore the girl's blouse from her shoulders. The slender woman didn't wear or need a bra.

"Now this looks interesting," Steve said.

Wind blown storm clouds unloaded, raced across the horizon. "No . . . no . . ." The girl whimpered, pounded her fists against the laughing broad's shoulders.

"See how easy it is, Mike?" She said to the driver.

Eyes wild, he drooled. Giggled when the girl's jeans were around her ankles. Howled when the thong pinched her thighs. She fell back. Mud squished under her butt.

"Come on, Mona," the big woman said. "Give me the rest of it."

"No!"

The woman lifted Mona's butt cheeks. "Oh . . ."

Her cry was like a dying animal's: so weak it was lost in the wind.

Growling, the attacker ripped the thong and the jeans past Mona's ankles. She heaved the garments into the street.

"Baby needs a spanking." The attacker was breathing hard.

Mouth wide in an unending scream, the naked woman protected her head, rolled to avoid the pummeling.

The rain gushed between her full breasts.

Her tapered belly rippled. The palm covering the shaved mound fell away.

Her cries quieted. Her hips thrashed. She squirmed, eyes glazed. Ten men and four women in jackets and great coats ran, laughing, from the diner.

Someone in the crowd yelled: "The bitch deserves a good spanking. "Is there any other kind?"

"That plump, round bottom needs to be jiggled," Mike wiped his lips.

His companion rubbed her hands. "That's what Mayor George Jay wants."

Jones pulled up his coat collar. Getting out, he showed the twelve gauge.

"Now folks, the lady's been hurt enough."

"She ain't no lady," the buxom woman said. "She's a misbehavin' cunt, is what she is."

"This is between the town and the bitch." The young man opened his jacket.

A three-fifty-seven was strapped to his chest, "Mine's bigger than yours." His laugh showed toothless jaws. Jones squeezed a round. The boom reverberated, whined when the slug tore a piece of blacktop near the young man's foot.

He jumped, stumbled into his companion's arms. The crowd retreated. "Ya see, son." Jones aimed at Mike's chest. "A fish with sharp gums is still a fish."

"Aw," Mike said.

Rain streaked his face. His eyelids fluttered. The plump woman glared. "She ain't worth the grief, trucker."

"Convince your partner, lady." Steve backed up to the driver's door.

Mona was gone. He reached for the door handle.

"I don't want any trouble, folks. This being my first visit to your delightful town."

Grumbling, they flicked their coat collars. From the other side of the street they watched him.

He pulled himself into the cab.

The cunt and underarm odors told him he was not alone.

"Carry passengers, trucker?" Mona forced a smile.

TWO

HE GAVE HER A BLANKET.

Outside Arnholt, he said: "Where to, lady?"

"Ma owns a farm the other side of Arnholt. About eleven miles. Before you get to Freemantle."

"Point it out."

"When we get there. Got a smoke?"

"Don't use 'em."

"I bet your kids are adopted, too."

"No kids."

He checked the rearview mirror; no traffic. "Thanks. For back there. Are you gay?"

"Not curious, either."

"Thing is, by next week, when old man Johnson gets the itch, he'll come looking like nothing ever happened. Wanna know what happened?"

"Nope."

"Pick up lots of naked pussy?"

"You're the first."

"You act like this happens all the time."

"I've picked up a few women who eventually got naked. When they climbed in they wore whatever they wore."

"Got man troubles?"

"Got a wicked boss. That's it."

"No, I mean . . ."

"I know what you mean."

"Tell me. I'm a registered nurse."

"I'm a licensed driver, a paid up member of the teamsters. Truck's had all her shots. I have the papers."

"Riding in an unlicensed rig's the least of my worries. Won't , . show myself in town unless I'm with Mayor Johnson. I'd love to spike his cocoa with rat poison."

"That'd fix him."

"That no good no-good."

"Will you be safe at your ma's?"

"She's a better shot than you, honey. Also an insomniac."

"Round the clock protection."

"Wanna stay over?"

"To do what?"

"Whatever."

"Some other time."

"Why haven't I seen you before?"

"Never been here before. Not since you were born."

"Why is that?"

"Your folks fucked when ma was ovulating."

"Yes, yes. That isn't what I meant."

"Detours are less hectic than wading through Arnholt."

"Not much to do here except eyeball the squack at the Up and Down Club. I dance there."

"When you're not healing the sick."

"I just said I was a nurse."

"Fooled me."

"I'd hate to do that."

The rain stopped. The moon appeared. Shadows danced in the ditches. She watched them.

"Our shack's more comfortable than shacking in back there." She moved closer. Her smell teased.

"We can get to know each other and I can thank you properly. I can give you a sample right here, or in back there."

"Do you like swollen jaws?"

"Bragging?"

"What's it sound like?"

"Strong, confident men. I love 'em."

"Not this one you won't."

"Not even for a night?"

"Depends on how nice your ma is."

"She's very nice. If she wasn't my ma, and I was so inclined, I'd drop my thong for her."

"I got a schedule."

"Otherwise?"

"Sure. Otherwise."

The mud packed ruts were topped with frost. The transport rolled through the muck like a weightlifter shouldering through a crowd. She dozed, woke, groaned. "Oh." She looked around. "Nearly there."

"Where?"

"See that four story on the hill? Over there. Barely see the roof through the elm. 'That ain't it. That's Johnson's shack. See that pasture a mile that way? Straight ahead and on the right. That's mine when she dies. Gate's around the curve."

"Where do I park?"

"Coming in?"

"Got to use the comforts."

"Park behind the house."

The house was gabled, two story, and a half acre wide. It faced the driveway.

"Ma collects those vans. You know the brand. The garage is full Drop it right there. Under the sentry light."

"I could lose the rig in your living room."

"Lost pa in there. Found his bones a year later." A tall husky woman in jeans and a flannel shirt stood in the back doorway. An AK-47 filled her hands.

"Is that your ma, or the sheriff."

"That's ma. She is the sheriff."

THREE

"WHO'S THE DUDE?"

"My savior, ma. From George shit's revenge."

"Told you to quit the club, or him."

"He owns the club. Not me."

The sheriff up and downed the trucker.

"What do I owe you, dude?"

"Five minutes in your drop zone."

"Big load, eh?" She winked.

"Two chili dogs too many."

"Come on, gasbag." Mona took Jones' hand.

Ten magazine reading minutes later he found the sheriff in the kitchen. She sat at the table, working the Omaha newspaper's jumble. The coffee pot percolated. The Russian AK leaned against the wall, within reach.

She looked up. "Mona's old man trucked from here to Idaho. Regular run. I know the importance of strong coffee."

He checked the wall clock. "I got time for a cup."

"Do you have time for a slice of homemade spiced apple pie to go with it."

"I always have time."

"How about Mona?"

"Too young. Too pretty. Too eager."

"Good answer."

She crossed to the counter, and the coffemaker and cups. Her butt cheeks rubbed together.

"Checking me out, trucker?" She filled a diner sized mug.

"Your ass was created for tight pants."

"Leg lifts created the distraction. Makes slipping the cuffs much easier than trying it in a loose one-piece. Cream? Sugar?"

"Straight. Like my ladies." He reached for the mug. Their fingers touched.

"Thanks for not dropping your digits where they're not wanted. Yet."

"I never feel-up the law."

She dropped muscular buttocks on the chair. "When you come through here again, stop by. Who knows what'll happen, mister . . ."

"Steve Jones."

"Grace Smith." She sipped, then said: "Twenty years since Mona's pa passed. Haven't slid stomachs in twenty years."

"Seven years since mine died."

"It gets easier."

"I heard that it does."

"Stop in again. Do it before the state weights and inspections catches you."

"How did you . . ."

"Why else would you detour through this country road of a town when the interstate's sanded, salted and plowed? By the way, Arnholt's weight limit is two tons. I could write you up, but won't."

"Already thanked me."

"Another cup?"

"Talk you out of a thermos worth?"

"Weather's still nasty."

"I got snows. And a schedule."

"Fried chicken. Garlic flavored mashed. Steamed okra. Coffee. Pie." She went to the hall. "Hey, daughter. Eats is on."

"I carry my own eat tools."

"Got plenty. Just move your ass a bit so I can set up."

She worked around him.

"Don't you and the mayor get along?"

"I work for him. I'm a flunky with a daughter he gets hard for. He holds mortgages on eighty percent of the land out here. Everyone's frightened of him."

"He's connected?"

She nodded. "He keeps Arnholt alive. Our economy is zero. New industry's the name of a rock band. George Johnson likes the quiet out here. His money keeps the diner open. The school open. The grocery store open. The subsistence checks handed out every Monday. With him gone this town would be the answer to the quiz question: whatever happened to Arnholt, Nebraska? No one messes with him. If anyone tries, well, what baby girl got is just his way of funning around. Mostly, his enemies wind up in shallow graves out there where the squirrels fart. Speaking of farts." She went to the hall. "Hey, baby girl. Tighten your robe. He isn't staying."

FOUR

OVER SECONDS OF PIE AND COFFEE, Grace said: "Why didn't you use your cell, child?"

"Mike Driscoll and his bitch jumped me as I headed for the car. I parked under a sentry light behind the club but was thinking my thoughts. About how I was gonna get back at the old man. I know everybody's afraid of him but, believe me, when he's laying there in his sweat and flab, and his cock won't lift, he whimpers and whines just like any old man."

"I heard that," Jones said.

"I doubt that." Mona nudged him.

"Every man's fear." Jones shook his head. "Sorry to say."

"Then don't say it," Mona said.

"So, child, they jumped you before you got to your car."

"Ma, I was at the car. Had the key in the door lock. They dropped a hood over my head. Took my purse. Drove to Main Street. Ever been stripped naked by high school drop outs?"

"No GEDs?" Jones said.

"Not one."

Grace said: "If I pull 'em in, child, will you file charges?"

"I like my face."

Jones cleared his throat. "How are you gonna make peace with him?"

"He got what he wanted," Grace said. "A graphic report from Driscoll and he will be satisfied. Baby girl? What happens if he cheats again?"

Mona shrugged. "I'd love to leave this cinder of a town. Let's both leave, ma."

"Go where? Do what?"

"I'd do stoop labor till you found something."

"Hon, my skills are using a gun, and the guts not to use it."

"Mine are ass shaking and dirty talking." She turned to Jones. "We've had this discussion before."

"Lots of befores," Grace said.

"My boss is always looking for drivers."

"What's his business?" Grace said.

"Unloading inventory."

"Illegals?"

"Whatever fits in a box and doesn't bitch when the lid's sealed."

"What's in your rig?"

"Curious? Or just being the sheriff?"

"Just wondering."

"I never ask."

"Afraid to know?"

"I back the rig to the loading dock. Unlock the double doors. While the warehouse crew loads up, I have a cup with the boss. He hands over the first half in cash, and the delivery address."

Mona pushed a box across the table. "Toothpick?"

"That question I can answer," he said.

"Here's another one. More coffee?"

After a refill, he said: "Well, ladies. Thanks for the eats and the jive."

"Let me check the road report." Grace left the room.

"Will you hate me if I make a move?"

"I got a load on."

"What's that mean?"

"I lost my wife."

"Already said."

"My gal pal."

She sighed. "I know."

"My sounding board."

"Ye gods and little fishes."

"The checkbook register's justifier."

Shaking her head, she stared at the ceiling.

"All in one chubby, redheaded package. All in one night. Since the old man with the bones grabbed Missus Jones and she slipped away one night when I was doing the road, well, kid, I just haven't done much in the slap and tickle department."

"Long haul between slides."

"Getting some place and getting back for a sweet twenty-four in the rack, with money in the bank. That's my life. And that's aw-right. Too much excitement's no good for a fifty year old."

"Waiting for the butcher to cut you down?"

"What gave it away?"

"What didn't? I know all about old men."

"Not as much as you think."

"Out there I didn't think. Next time I'll do the dance differently."

Her eyes were cold. She blushed. Her lips and legs tightened.

"He fucks stray stuff, I will do likewise. Someone just passing through town. Get it?"

He pushed away from the table. "I never pee in another man's pot. If I was looking, it'd be for a woman without a partner."

"Do you like ma?"

"I sure could."

"Pencil her in for home cooking and in-bed snooking."

"Depends on her."

"When there's a man she wants to impress she does this little ass wiggle. Last one she wiggled for was pop. She's wet and wanting it. Did you get it?"

"Full in the face."

"That's not where it was intended."

"I got it there."

"Wet stones?"

"Slightly damp."

"I'd drown you." She got up. "With this bod I don't beg."

She cupped her breasts. "These bad girls get men and some women in a drooling mood."

Grace returned.

"I'm depressed, ma."

"Why?"

"He won't play." Mona pouted.

"Good grief, child. Who spiked the coffee with pity pills?"

"Just reaching out, ma."

"Keep reaching, baby girl. Here's the latest road report."

He put on drug store readers.

"If you can't read my scrawl, every road and the interstate west are frozen. Sand and salt rigs waiting till the rain stops. Around midnight, they think. Most likely you'll be trapped here till then."

"Can you tolerate my stink another two hours?"

"Don't your snow tires work?" Mona furiously filed her nails.

"I'm worried about the civilians without snows."

Grace said: "Guest room's upstairs."

Mona scowled. "Yes, Stevie. There's even an inside lock on the door."

"Sorry, Steve. It must be her time."

"She doesn't even know for sure when that is."

"I can sleep in the rig."

"House arrest. Till dawn. And you, child, behave."

"I will," she whispered.

"Be sure that you do."

"Would I lie to the sheriff?"

"All the time."

Steve stretched. "Excuse me while I set the alarm and tracker."

"A big one, isn't he?" Mona tongue teased saliva.

"Six four in bare feet and I always wear sox."

"I wonder if the joint's open?"

Mona took the cell into the hall. "Need anything? If you stay over."

"I carry what I need in the coat pocket."

Mona returned.

"Jesse said all the broads are down there. My VW hasn't been boosted."

"Need a lift?"

"Ma has four wheel drive. A lotta four wheel drives."

"Why don't we all go?" Grace said. "Stay with her while she works, bring her home." He yawned.

"Why can't she phone in sick?"

"I like doin' the act. I want you to see it."

"Ah, hell," he said. "Why not?"

FIVE

WHEN THEY ENTERED the Up and Down Club, the bartender plugged in the juke box. The four women, on the fat side of forty, mounted the stage.

They listlessly hip swayed, hoisted sagging breasts, flicked the corklike nipples. Above the thongs, their bellies jiggled. Belly buttons became deep circles that flattened when their belly flab tightened. Their thighs bounced. Flaccid asscheeks rotated. One dancer chewed gum. Another stared at a spot above the bar. The other patted her partner's ass; her partner shook her off.

"Waiting to die is how they look," Steve said.

"What's needed is Mona time." She tossed her coat, kicked off her boots, changed the song to the uptempo *Nasty Girls*.

"When I start jiving, Jesse," she said to the bartender, "remember to drop the volume so the crowd can hear me."

The old woman's laugh was raspy and ended with a cough.

After the first chorus Mona threw the signal; the volume dropped. She undid her bra. The nipples on the swollen spheres lifted. The other dancers stopped.

Mona winked at Steve. He shuttered his eyes.

"Like my titties? I know you do. I see all them tables levitating. Don't rock on right yet, fellers. Wait till ya see what else there is."

She peeled the thong, tossed it. Grace caught it.

"Wet already." Grace wiped her palms on her jeans.

"I've seen all of her already," Steve said. The sheriff shushed him.

"Do that turn, Mona." With extended index finger, Grace did an air turn. "Like I taught you."

Hips swiveling, Mona turned, faced her guests.

"Mmmm, a storm's churning in my cunt. A scalding, surging inferno and, oh, oh, ouch." Her eyelids tightened. She grimaced. "Ow, ow, wow, the storm's broke." She spread her labia. "Oh, look." Wide eyed amazement. She held herself open. "Oh, boys, have ya ever seen a clean, pink pussy like this one? Tighter than a school girl. Needs something thick and hard to pierce it, spread it wide open and slam into it till it's all red and wet and, oh, oozing." Her voice dropped. "Uh, so deep. No one to thrash it and, look-eeee here, that throbbing little thumb smaller than a baby's thumb, and so ready to give me so much pleasure. See all that cum, fella?" She shook her business in Steve's face. "Look it. Lick it."

He scooted away from the stage.

"Coward." Her laugh sounded like a rusty cowbell.

At the stage apron she squatted, showing the moles in her deep cleavage. Her vagina's muskiness thickened, spread. The juke box screamed.

She gasped, wild eyed, neck veins taut, flinging spit from the corners of her pouting mouth. The expression was corpselike.

"I taught her how to survive. Do you hate me, Steve?"

His knee bumped the table. "Got her keys?"

"I thought you were keeping me company?"

"The place stinks, like what killed my wife. How it was before she passed."

"Meet us at the diner." She rummaged through her purse. "Unless business picks up, her set'll be short. Sixty-five minutes, tops."

"What's her bus look like?"

"Red VW. You saw it." She tossed the keys.

"Hey, Stevie," Mona yelled over the music. "Wait'll ya see what I do with Jesse's tongue."

The bartender was down to her red lace bra.

He coughed, spat.

He began scraping the VW's windshield.

When Margo died, with the cell phone filling her hand, he was getting head from a truckstop hooker. His cell was off. She died alone.

Earlier, she tried to reach his father; his number appeared on the speed dial but not on the caller ID.

Ten minutes later he inched along the highway into Arnholt. The diner's neon flickered.

Steve and the cook had the place to themselves.

Steve ordered a short stack and coffee.

The husky, middle-aged woman poured two cups.

"Fresh?" he said.

"Seasoned."

"That only works with whiskey."

"I wouldn't know. I don't drink."

He took a sip. "This'll keep my bowels open."

"Strong coffee is like a strong broad. Makes you glad you're a man."

"I don't get it."

"Would you like to?"

"No offense."

"None taken. I'm a pro." She took her cup into the kitchen. "Don't worry. The cakes'll fill your cavity even if you won't fill mine."

A copy of the Arnholt County Chronicle was within reach.

Nothing new in the world. Nothing he cared about.

"What's with the weather?" he said.

"Gonna be a bitch and three fourths. Last bulletin. By April the roads'll be passible."

"I figured that."

"Figured you did."

"Were you around when that girl was stripped?"

"I'm always here."

"What was that about?"

"About Arnholt breaking the boredom. When suicide's the main topic of conversation, anything works."

"They stage regular stripathons?"

"Planning your vacation?"

"No plans for anything."

"They only happen when old man Satan says so."

"The mayor?"

"Yep. He sits in his house on the hill with a telescope and his cock while we do all the work."

"What keeps you on your feet?"

"What I'm doin' now." From an apron pocket she took a syrup dispenser. "Refill?"

"Unless you got something else to do."

"I was expecting a smarter give-back."

"Best I can do on short notice."

She refilled her cup. "Well, long legs."

"How're the griddlers coming?"

"Can't eat 'em raw."

"Sure can't."

"What about you?"

"I don't taste too good raw."

"Bet you do. But who's betting? Tell me about yourself."

"I drive a truck."

"I know that. Where ya from? Where ya heading?"

"I'm from everywhere. Nowhere. Aiming west. Wanna lift?"

"These boobies can sure use hoisting. But that's not what you're talking about."

"Tits look fine. Only don't shame yourself by showing up at a topless contest."

"How about a bottomless bump and grind?"

"I like big-assed babes."

"My back talent's too ripe for hiding. Which is why I don't wear a girdle. Why hold 'em down and be uncomfortable?"

"Give the customers something to live for."

"Keeps me going, And coming." She leaned. "If ya get my meaning."

He ignored the view.

"Tell me about the trucker with no name."

"That's the whole story."

"Not from around here?" She went back to the griddle. "Lived around here for a time. Lived elsewhere."

"There's something about you that's familiar."

"Been told I look like what's his name. Eastman."

"Eastwood."

"Him, too."

"Only Eastman I know is this cunt who vanished with my heart and forty bucks from the till." She turned the cakes.

"Love's a bitch."

"She sure was. More poison?"

"Might as well."

Her perfume covered the sweat. She breathed onion breath in his face.

"Why'd you do what you did? Out there."

"I was looking to try out my new twelve gauge. Slobber jaws and his pussy looked like decent targets."

"They ain't decent."

"Guessed that."

"They're what the word 'loser' was created for."

"They must be tight with the mayor."

"They work for him. Do little shit for him." He took out his lower plate.

"Mind?" he lisped.

"I can see it's yours. Who else's would it be?"

"Don't sell the place while I'm gone." He went to the mens room.

When he returned, she said: "Yeah, trucker, Arnholt's the end of the horizon. No gold pot here. Just a privy overflowing with lost innocence and blunted hope."

"Like ma always said: we're born, we suffer, we die."

"Ain't it sad?" She checked on the griddlers. "It's all we have."

"Not much."

She ran a damp rag along the narrow counter top.

"Smells like teen spirit. Or griddlers ready for chomping."

She slid the cakes onto a large, chipped plate.

"More poison, please."

"Tempting your bladder."

"I don't, then who else will?"

She held the plate by its rims.

"Eat 'em before they eat you."

He held the syrup dispenser above the plate. He kept the spout closed.

"What?" she said. "Something wrong with 'em?"

"With my head."

"Wanna codeine cap?"

"Bad memory. Not a headache."

"Like that flying elephant: I'm all ears, pappy."

"I never forgot my first lay. Then I hit forty, and I did forget."

"Someone forgot my phone number."

"I was fourteen. I wasn't allowed to use the phone."

"What did you think? That first fuck would last to old age?"

"Vicki Dunham." A rueful smile.

"If you ever get the need you know where I am. If not behind the counter, then the bone yard. More sludge?"

"Half cup to wash it down."

"You're all hunched over. Back?"

"Bone density loss. Brittle, like my sense of humor."

He checked the clock above the counter.

"Waiting, or bored?"

"Waiting."

"I will let you finish in peace. If you need anything." She pointed at the griddle. "I will be up to my armpits in grease."

He wiped syrup with the last pancake.

"Taste good?" she said at the grill.

"Better than good."

"Syrup helps."

"Cold weather gooses the appetite."

"Any week with a Saturday gooses mine."

"On you it looks good."

"Why, thank you. What does?"

"A healthy appetite."

"Guys and some gals liked to roll me around, humping my belly before gravitating to the lower region."

"Plump women are usually real tight."

"All that flab shifts. I also tighten up. And try not to take on too many fellas with oak trees between their legs."

"We'd be perfect together."

"Deprived, as I remember. And scarred, if memory serves."

"I do what I can with what I got."

"I remember that, too."

He finished what was in the cup. "When you're waiting life goes on and on."

"I'm open till three."

"I won't wait that long."

"Might not have to."

Vicki looked beyond him to the figure at the door. Grace came in, with the wind and Mona behind her.

"Thought I forgot you?"

"Jiving with a grade school chum."

"Can I interest you ladies in fresh perked?"

"Yeah."

"Sure."

She waddled toward the percolator.

Vicki filled two cups, served them at the counter.

"Straight or with extras?"

"Straight up," they said. Grace dug in her purse.

"No charge. I know you. Did not know you were friends of my old school chum, old what's his name?"

"Someone doesn't make an impression." Mona stirred coffee.

Wind rattled the window.

"Storm's coming," Vicki said.

"Sounds like it's here." Steve took out his money clip.

"Sounds like it." Mona emptied the cup in two swallows. She exhaled steam.

A roach crossed the kitchenside counter edge. Steve thumbed twenties until he found a five dollar bill.

"We better be going," Grace said. "Before it strands us."

"Plenty of room upstairs, girls."

Mona gave the cook a fast up and down. "Thanks, awfully."

"Noel Coward lives," Vicki said under her breath. Steve dropped the fiver on the counter.

Vicki folded the bill. "Stop in for breakfast. Meet all the lost souls."

The crease sliced Mr. Lincoln's face in half. Goodbyes, and the door closed behind them. Vicki dropped the bill in the money drawer. She waited until the cars skidded from the curb.

She went to the landline wall phone.

"Mr. Johnson, this is Vicki Dunham. Someone you should know about. Oh, you already do."

SIX

ABANDONED ON BOTH SIDES of main street were 1970s and 80s pickups and SUVs. The gas station at block's end had a "closed until spring" sign above the four pumps.

Jones rode in the van. The VW stayed a car's length behind. Their headlights stabbed the darkness.

"My little minx gets off flashing herself," Grace said. "Even if it's to her old ma and a bunch of life-sufferers who barely remember what goes on and off in bed."

They approached the final intersection before the exit out of Arnholt. The wind picked up. The single overhead traffic signal shuddered.

The road was deserted. The drizzle was replaced by fog.

"I really don't know what to do about her," she said.

An open-handed gesture. "Me and mine never had kids."

"A curse or a comfort. Depending."

From the other side of the county the Amtrak horn punctuated the irregular clicks of moisture from low-hanging elm.

"When I hear one of those, Steve, I want to be in a sleeper out of Arnholt, out of Nebraska, out of the midwest. Away from my obligations. I don't have the drop downs."

The van bounced on the rutted toad. Farm sentry lights wavered. Headlights swept the ditch edges. Ahead, the driveway lights up the hill to Johnson's front door pebbled the mist. The four stories were dark.

"I have this feeling, Steve, that the old man is sitting up there, in the dark, scoping the town through a night vision rig. Creeps me out."

"Leave."

"Who would take care of her?"

"Any guy who can tolerate her."

"Not many are willing. Oh, there have been a few. Mike Driscoll kept her on his pig farm until Della Plove showed up. Mona humped her in the shower. Mike caught them. There were others."

"Mama's the buffer and the doormat."

"She's the only family I have."

"Ma died just before the wife. I took care of ma, then the wife."

"Now it's the rig and the road?"

"The whole equation." A shrill beeping from his coat pocket.

"What's that? An angry mouse?"

"The tracker!"

SEVEN

THE SEMI WAS GONE.

The tracking device beeped.

From Grace's kitchen he phoned Omaha.

Omaha Harry Lance answered on the second ring.

"Some genius dismantled the alarm, Harry. The rig is still in the four hundred mile radius."

"Where are you?"

Steve told him. "Is Nick available?"

"Soon as he gets his jockeys on."

He gave directions. Meet him at the diner."

Mona filed her toenails. Grace ignored the cup of coffee she'd just poured.

"Harry, he'll need four wheel drive and snows."

"He has both."

"Two hours?"

"Two and a half."

Steve headed for the door.

"Wait."

"I can't."

Grace unlocked the gun cabinet. "You can." He reached for the Russian AK and shells.

"Here's the plan, Steve, I follow in the van. You drive the VW. When we get to where we have to go I stay. You pick up. You chase the jackers. I come along as a rep of the law. Make sense?"

"Let's go."

The temp was thirty degrees. Their breath burst and died. They picked their way to the garage.

"Around here who's smart enough to dismantle a truck alarm?"

"Della Plove."

"Driscoll's cunt."

"There aren't any others smart enough and skilled enough."

"Where do I find her?"

"His pig farm. Down the road and a mile west. Then south one mile. "Is the place rigged with cameras?"

"No. I make routine sweeps through the county. If he has cameras or some other system I don't know about it."

Jones drove west. The signal got louder. He turned south. The macadam crunched. The fog swallowed their headlight's glow.

He opened the window. She was two car lengths behind.

The wind cooled his face, but couldn't flush the pig waste stink. Fields like women, spread and waiting, to elm copse a mile away. A half mile beyond that, a farm house with lights burning.

The elm grove was on the other side of the road. The two lane wood ramp over the ditch rattled. The VW's snow tires hit the iced surface.

He parked behind the copse. She stopped behind him. "Here." She gave him pocket-sized binoculars. He squinted at the two story frame at the end of the macadam access road. Behind worn curtains on the first floor front window, the lights gave the window jagged eyes, "See anything?"

"Can't see much with them." He gave them back. "Not from here."

"I have a flashlight but the battery's low. Meant to buy a new one but didn't feel like driving two miles in this weather to Freemantle."

He looked at her.

When she paused for breath, he said: My night vision's good. Any traps between here and there?"

"Pot holes. No sink holes."

He checked his watch. "If I'm not back here by two take off for the diner. Look for a four wheel drive with Douglas County plates. Don't tell him you're the law. He gets real shaky around strangers. After I reconnoiter, I'll wait here. If I'm not, go there."

"Good luck. Or do you want something more?"

"I'd like to be forty again. With my Margo, waiting with a hot meal and a hot mattress. I'd settle for the mattress."

"I can do both."

He strapped the AK forty-seven to his shoulder. He shoved the shells in the coat's deep pockets.

"Let me come with you."

"Nick Gray. The diner."

She got back in the van.

When he was beyond ear shot, she said: "Damn fool."

EIGHT

THE FOG EMBRACED HIM. With each step, he shivered. The cold penetrated his bones.

A quarter mile from the objective the fog broke into clusters. Moon slivers guided him to the gate.

A scan of the gate posts and two elm on either side of the drive showed smooth steel and rumpled bark.

The gate was unlocked. He listened for attack dogs.

It was quiet enough to hear squirrels fart.

The AK at port arms he dog trotted up the two lane driveway. The coat hem slapped his ankles. His boots, scraping the pebbles imbedded in the macadam made "kronk kronk" sounds.

He veered from the open porch to the nearest window. Through a curtain gap: a ragged overstuffed couch, a recliner, two facing armchairs, a coffee table between them, and, on the far end, an alcove with a table and chairs. The kitchen was beyond that. A shadow flitted against the sink.

The semi was parked on the other side of the two story frame. The double doors were open. A ramp led from the gravel parking space to the back end. Someone came through a basement door. Jones couldn't see the door. He heard it.

Driscoll went to the truck. His tossed cigarette shot sparks.

He wore a padded jacket, stocking cap, work gloves. He turned toward the shadows where Jones hid. Snot covered his upper lip. Without teeth the lip sagged. He needed a shave, a wash up.

He went up the ramp, into the truck.

A moment later, a motor fired. A rising and falling, grinding noise of a two-pronged fork lift got louder as the two-wheeler rumbled down the ramp. Balanced on the prongs was an oblong box ten feet long and two feet wide. The container was lashed to the prongs.

The basement door opened.

The storage area must be close. Over the two-wheeler's noise he heard the door.

The vehicle disappeared. A softer barely audible sound of the fork lift passing over smooth cement almost covered Driscoll's: "Git yer sweet ass outta the way." A female giggle.

The vehicle stopped. A brief pistoning as the prongs dropped.

A snuffling noise when the box was stacked on another box. Then the fork lift's high pitch as it turned toward the door.

Jones stayed in place until the two-wheeler drove deeper into the basement. It was a low ceilinged room running the length of the house. The rows of large oblong storage crates and boxes along the three walls dwarfed the interior.

Della Plove had her back to the open door. She held a clipboard and a ballpoint. She checked each container against the cargo manifest.

They didn't realize the trucker was there until Driscoll turned the fork lift.

Jones aimed at the boy's nose. Driscoll killed the ignition.

Della dropped the clipboard.

"Show your fists. Over your head."

The gusts blew dust devils.

The manifest rattled against the clipboard.

"Both of you. Strip. Toss your clothes behind you. Anything flies at me you'll be flying."

Mike shuddered.

Della's giggle pinched her throat.

"Can I explain something?" Driscoll unzipped his jacket.

"I'm drowning in bullshit, son."

She dropped her gloves, cap and ankle length fur lined coat.

"Shit heel."

"Say it louder for Omaha, which is where you're going."

Fatigue pounded. His eyes burned.

"This is a mistake, mister." Driscoll dropped his shirt.

"Yours." Jones steadied the weapon.

She balled the flannel shirt. "Don't waste energy, Mike."

"You're gonna need it." Jones licked dry lips.

Whimpering, the boy stepped away from his jeans. He wore an undershirt and jock strap.

"Them, too." Jones aimed at the boy's groin.

Driscoll did what he was told.

"Where's your jolly roger?" Jones took shallow breaths to keep from coughing.

"My what?"

"I didn't think you had one."

"Where's yours?" She pinched her nipples. "Oh, oh. Are you hard, mister? Didn't think so. Admit it, cock bitch. You can't make the move."

"What's happening here, kids, so you can write it right in your blogs." Jones couldn't feel his toes. "This is what you earned yesterday."

"Or is it to see if you got the marrow to fill your stones?"

The chill thickened her nipples. The gray, goose-fleshed caps blushed, hardened.

"For a big broad, I'm solid." She peeled the thong.

Jones tapped his toes. Heat surged through his soles, ankles.

Under the ceiling lights glare her thick bush sparkled. Tiny diamonds slickened the mound, upper thighs, lower stomach roll.

Her odor teased his nostrils. His eyes watered. He bit his tongue to keep from sneezing.

"If, truck jock, you can't raise it for normal play, how about this way?" Hips swivelling, she turned. Her supple hind melons bounced. Plump. Blemishless. Like Margo's.

When she turned her belly rippled. The navel was an O-shaped crater.

"Please, mister."

The wind whipped. The walls squeaked. The couple shivered.

"The keys." Jones tasted blood.

"My pocket." Driscoll massaged his upper arms.

Her breasts lifted, lowered with each breath. "I hope we're here to see how this wraps."

"It'll wrap with you promising never to fuck over an over the road jockey."

"Let me explain." Driscoll thrust shaking hands.

"Make it like your prick."

"We were ordered to rip you."

"From the man on the hill." She popped a cleavage pimple.

Her stomach rippled. She farted. A long loud burst that the outside wind couldn't dissipate.

"Oh, excuse it. Terribly unladylike." She made a grotesque face.

"Whew! Smells like fried rat tails."

"That's the high point of my day," Mike said. "Hearing you fart, matching the tone and intensity. The variety of sound. The pipe organ effect. Hoping for potent rectal perfume to match yours, my love."

Jones' coat collar pinched. He unbuttoned it.

"If you boys wanna encore, keep the gun pointed at my pussy."

Jones knew the answer, but asked the question: "Why is the old man on me?"

"Because you are stupid." Her teeth clicked.

"We don't know." Shoeless, Driscoll did a one-step dance in place.

"Or care." She shook like a prick over a urinal.

"Doesn't matter. Find the keys. Bring them over."

"Here," Mike said a moment later.

"Now." Jones pocketed them.

"Now what?" Her skin glistened.

"The long march."

"Uh-oh." Her belly spasmed. "Here it comes, boys."

"Oh, you wouldn't." Mike's voice jumped an octave.

"When a girl has to fart, she just has to and I just did."

"So silent, dear. So subtle."

"Git!"

'Bastard." She quivered.

Her smell, like a moist breath on his groin, raised Jones erection.

Mike whined. "Can we negotiate?"

"I know you can. I'm sure you will." He stepped aside.

They went out.

"He will castrate you."

The wind burst against her shoulders. She groaned, gagged. Mike sobbed.

"Dammit, Mike, get your manhood on." She ran past Driscoll.

"Move it!" Jones goosed Driscoll with the muzzle.

"Oh, oh." Driscoll stumbled. His shoulder and the rig collided. She cleared the side of the house. Screaming, wailing, she sprinted down the drive. She danced over the rocks.

Then, suddenly:

"Dammit. Stop. Both of you. Get back here."

Her bloody soles traced her return. Mike massaged his shoulder.

"Inside." Where he said: "Plan change. Get dressed. Reload, Don't break nothin'. I see armor I kill you."

"Thank you." Mike swallowed a sob.

"Yeah, go screw yourself."

An hour to reload.

How was he going to do that toilet thing with these two still healthy?

If his partner, Arnie Barnes was here he would do what he did best. Jones couldn't pull a trigger.

He went outside for a breath of air that didn't stink of sweat and cunt. From where he stood he saw them. His back faced the truck.

Boots scuffed gravel. Before he turned a sawed off's muzzle touched his neck.

"Party's over," the old man said. "Hello, son."

"Hello, fuck daddy."

NINE

MIKE AND DELLA DRESSED and went upstairs. The mayor and the trucker faced across the coffee table.

Johnson said: "Mike, Della, I decided to send the boodle to the west coast after all. Might as well get the money. Thaw out. Reload. Junior needs product to show the buyer."

"Then you take it back," Jones said.

Johnson's gaze remained on his son. "Got some marrow in your bones?"

"Some."

Della massaged Mike's back. He pulled away.

"Mister Johnson. Mister, mayor. Sir boss. We didn't sign on to do stoop labor."

"A little late with the testosterone," she said. "The only one here with a fuck stick is Mr. Mayor."

Johnson beamed. "I will take my bow sitting down."

Which he did.

"Did you enjoy the drama out there, George?" Della said.

"It was dramatic, wasn't it?"

"In a nudie sort of way." She licked her upper lip.

"Sure was." Mike trembled.

Johnson's smile was gone.

"Stoop labor? That's what you said? Don't you look at your pay checks?"

"Yes, but."

"The truck needs to be reloaded."

Mike and Della fled down the back stairs.

"What is this? Overdue family time? Do I drop my pants and bend over?"

"That happened once. How many times must I apologize?"

"Every time I look down I remember the barbed wire."

"Got you potty trained."

"Got me a dozen stitches down there. I can't hose like most men."

"A big cock breaks the natural drape of custom cut suit pants."

"Never wore a suit."

"Buried your wife in work clothes?" Johnson plucked a nostril hair. "How long has she been gone. Five years?"

"Seven."

"Enough about her. What I have to tell you is this." A dramatic pause. "I'm about to control the world!"

"Mind if I shit first?"

TEN

JOHNSON SIPPED FRESH BREWED COFFEE. "How'd it come out?"

"The normal way."

"I've never needed a laxative."

"Good."

"Not impressed?"

"Not much."

The old man gestured at the carafe and the mug next to it. "Best bowel flusher there is."

Jones yawned. "Ouch."

"Girdle too tight?"

"I yawn too hard and my spine cracks."

"Self pity?"

"Statement of fact."

"Thought you had some marrow in your bones."

"No marrow. No curiosity."

"Before you go on your uninformed journey west you should know what you're transporting. Those boxes and crates? The elements of an atom smasher."

Jones looked in the mug for foreign substances.

"How much do you know about God's particles?"

"Nothing."

"Without God's particles the universe couldn't be joined to form mass. The atom smasher creates this phenomenon. How I obtained what you will truck to the west coast doesn't need explaining."

"I get paid. That's all I care about."

"Should I sell it or construct it? Make Arnholt the leader of the scientific community, or resell the parts? At first, the former. Which is why I hired those children you shamed.

After they boosted the truck I decided to embrace the money. Keep the parts and resell them. Wake up!"

"I am."

"Are you?"

Steve raised a hand. "See? I'm awake. I'd better be. Seeing as how I'm sharing space with a viper."

"I could do you damage." He snapped his fingers. "Like that."

He massaged his thumb and index finger.

"Already did!"

"Not that Margo thing again?"

"You respected your pumping hand more than you respected her. That's why she crawled into my bed."

"In my own way I loved her."

"Treating her like a whore was not the way."

"That's what she was. I took her off mattress patrol. Took her everywhere. Paid for the abortions. Dammit, I was the villain because I couldn't make her scream in high 'C'. That was my crime."

"Faulty heart valves weakened her. Cancer killed her."

"I might have paid for the surgery. You couldn't. That's your crime."

"I loved her. Still do."

"Love isn't the only four-letter word."

"Her last night. She couldn't reach me. She called you. Why would she do that?"

"Perhaps it was to obtain my chili recipe. Still a favorite?"

"No."

"She killed that."

"Cholesterol numbers killed that."

"Lean beef's the secret."

"I like my beef fatter than a carnival stripper's ass."

"I liked broad-beamed broads. Like punching an angora lined pillow."

"Potty training almost killed my cunt hunger."

"Was she your gal pal confessor?"

"She deep-sixed the depression."

Johnson leaned back. "She had this technique. An old man's position, she called it. Seizing my cock tip between her teeth she used her tongue. When it was good as I could make it, she clenched the tip with her pussy lips. A slow back and forth brought out the troops. Get it?"

"Got it. I brought her through those heavenly gates, with my tongue."

"I never put it there."

"She was clean. Appreciative."

"A woman's orgasm? A woman's chin music."

"Your money and what comes with it and you couldn't bring her off."

"Can you bring it off? Get their money and get gone and live to spend your cut? Can you bring it off?"

"What's my walk-away?"

"One hundred thousand, plus air fare to wherever you wanna live."

"For that kind of pocket change I can walk fast."

"It might be more. If I can cut expenses."

"Who gets pink slipped?"

"Why do you need to know?"

"You're right."

"Since I'm not assembling the unit I don't need that fat ass Plove and that fat head Driscoll."

Jones stood.

"Leaving so soon?"

"The rig's probably ready." He started for the back stairs.

"Give me a minute.I will give you answers."

"Nothing you do surprises me. That's the answer."

"A moment." Johnson thumbed four twenties from the platinum money clip. "Here." He dropped them on the table.

"My birthday was last month."

"Pick them up."

Steve did. "Now can I go?"

"Allow me to feed my ego."

"Is that another name for attack dog?"

"Sit. Please."

Steve folded the money on his brass clip.

"'That strip-a-rama yesterday. Mona's gotten uppity. She won't give me what I have to get. The bareass follies were for her, plus guerilla theater for the masses."

"That was improv for the civilians?"

"The state cops and the welfare agencies know what's going on here. Every month they receive donations from Arnholt Social Services. The acronym?"

"How did I get this haul?"

"Omaha Harry Lance is a friend. He tipped me. We were on your tracking frequency. When Plove dismantled the alarm she left the tracker operational."

The old man filled his cup. His hand was steady.

"Can I go now?"

"Are you still here?"

At the foot of the stairs Steve bumped into Doctor Driscoll. He wore dentures. He fell back, arms flailing. He and the wall collided.

"Nice chops." Jones rushed past. "Lose the real ones in prison?"

"I lost my teeth and my heart at Carnegie Tech."

Della resealed a box. "What you forced us to do cranked my crank."

"Part of my neighborly service."

"The keys are in the ignition."

Her crotch stink followed him out.

When the truck was loaded she tapped on the window. He woke up.

He wondered where Grace and Nick were.

ELEVEN

Two AM.

Jones dropped the clutch in granny low. The studs cracked the ice layers.

The brittle sound awakened a squirrel.

It leaped from the garbage bags piled in the alley between the diner and a vacant storefront.

The vehicles were parked at the curb.

The street was deserted.

The diner's neon flickered, buzzed. Vicki Dunham dozed at the counter. No sign of Grace or Nick.

He parked in front of the diner. The air brakes engaging woke the cook.

She waved, grinned, coughed.

"Can't get enough of my wonderful stuff, trucker?" She rubbed her eyes.

"Looking for the sheriff and her kid."

"The pair you left with."

"Seen either one since the last time?"

"Just the last time."

"I lost 'em."

"Still lost, hon, cause I ain't seen either one. Coffee ain't fresh. It'll open your eyes and your bowels, though. Are ya game?"

"No game." He dropped on a stool. "How deep are you in this?"

"In this . . .what?"

"Mayor's cathouse on wheels."

"Not familiar with no traveling trick turners."

"The Mayor's running a scam. Know anything about that?"

"How could I not know?"

"Then you do?"

"I do not. I lived here all my life. I never left home. When Johnson settled here he knew my folks.. When he ran for mayor I hung his campaign posters on that wall over there. When he sponsored public forums he held 'em here. I made the coffee and billed him for it and he paid promptly. He stops in every so often for a cup, and conversation, and other things, too. When he hands out those subsistence checks he does it right here. The city-county building has mold and a bat infestation. This place is, temporarily, the mayor's office. Right over there by the space heater is where the issues get discussed and solved. I'd know if something odd was going on. It isn't."

"Did you snitch me out?"

She flinched, said: "Who would I snitch you to?"

"Mayor Johnson knew I was here."

"Not many big rigs come through Arnholt. Pour a cup?"

"My kidneys couldn't take it." He eased off the stool.

His lower back and hips pounded.

"If I see who you're looking for I'll tell her."

He grunted something. The door swung shut behind him.

The wind kicked. Squirrels chattered. Behind the trash bags rats clamored.

"Not gonna get me just yet, fellas."

He adjusted the Russian AK.

His father deserved retribution.

It wasn't Steve's to give.

TWELVE

TWO THIRTY.

Jones parked behind Grace's house.

The sentry light across the drive showed the vans in the garage.

Nick Gray's van was between the VW and the sheriff's van.

Lights upstairs went on.

Grace met him at the back door. "I suppose you're wondering."

Her ungirdled belly strained the tattered robe.

"Made friends real fast, Grace."

She started down the hall. Her thighs rubbed, whispered, mocked the truck jockey.

In the front room a corner lamp was on the lowest setting.

"Nick and I have known each other since Mona was a pup. Coffee? Something stronger?"

He placed the rifle under the coffee table.

"We thought you'd be dead or converted by now." Nick filled the doorway. The flannel shirt dropped below the hip holster.

Jones hand dropped.

"Don't."

"My ass needs scratching."

"Scratch and sit."

The couch's hard backrest soothed Steve's lower spine.

"Here's why I'm here."

"I called you."

"That, and more."

"I found it." He thumbed at the window facing the drive.

"The and-more? I'm back up. If you get your back up and decide to do some dealing on your own I prevent that."

The forced smile showed newly capped teeth.

"The old man convert you?"

"To what?"

"Didn't he give you the talk?"

Grace left the room.

"We talked. Personal shit."

"He told you about the haul?"

"All about that."

"In? Out? Which?"

"I'm here. The cargo's there. What's the plan, man?"

"I take care of the buyers. In LA."

"Pick up loose change on Wilshire Boulevard."

"Whatever I can."

"Harry's in on this?"

"Up to his fat cheeks."

"I'm in on it. Or out of it."

"Way out of it."

"Got me by the short shank."

"A few more Franklins in your pay envelope."

A pause. Then:

"When do we leave?"

The hall toilet flushed. Grace came down the hall.

"For an old sow she's great nookie," Nick said. "Already know that?"

"Never had the pleasure."

"It always is. Well, pardner, kick back. Wake you around eleven."

"Eleven's fine." Jones unlaced his boots, kept them on.

"Sleep with them on?"

"I keep my chops in a side pocket. No teeth would be embarrassing.

"With no chops you look stupid. No boots, well, that's a problem. Mona's another one. If you don't stick it to her you're aw-right. She has the death sentence. Bat I wasn't talking about her. I was talking about other drivers."

"In twenty five years not a scratched fender."

"After this is over you can take a vacation. We got buyers with deep pockets for when the current owners do their exit."

"Long way to LA."

"Not that far."

"Side trips. To beat the inspectors."

"We don't have a lotta time."

"I know how to do the dodge."

Gray nodded. "How do ya like your eggs?"

"Out of the chicken."

Jones stretched out.

He woke up to a pussy smell.

"Breakfast, sweetie. Right now." Mona straddled his face.

"Judas."

Gripping her naked ass he lifted her, dropped her between the couch and coffee table.

"What's the time?"

"Eleven. Coffee's percolating."

"Save it for the marines."

"Marines? Oh-oh-oh."

"Just an expression, dear." Grace placed a mug on the table. "Eggs, bacon, griddle cakes in the kitchen."

"My smeller has been compromised."

"She has that effect."

Jones coughed.

"Please, don't." Mona ran to the hall. "Swine flu."

"Got that, too?"

"What do you mean?"

"Nothing." Jones' finger combed thinning gray hair. Dirt crusted, jagged nails snagged a few strands. He flicked the strands.

"I got a flu shot, Stevie. Wanna see where?"

"Seen it. Nobody's perfect."

Mona's impish grin died.

"Yesterday I thought you were." Her eyes darkened. Her breasts sagged.

"I really thought you were, Steve."

"Well, I am Steve. Not perfect."

"I know you're Steve."

A sly grin ignited the fire in her eyes.

"Steve with a frayed sleeve."

"Thrift shop threads."

"Frayed rhymes with laid."

"Nick's around." His hand, when he embraced the mug, trembled.

"His tongue's up mama's silk purse."

Using both hands he guided the mug to his lips.

"Coffee nerves?"

"Job stress."

The warmth felt good going down.

"Me, as well. Piles from too much ass-working." She slapped her ass. The cheeks wobbled.

"Take it up there?"

"If, by up there, you mean the club. Yes. If you mean do I let them stick it there, the answer is no. My blow hole's tighter than a schoolboy's fist. You a butt breaker?"

"I can't afford it."

"If you could?"

"I'd eat steak and let the ladies eat hamburger."

"I smell breakfast."

"I smell unwashed cunt."

She pouted. "Am I that gross?"

"Ripe. Not gross."

"Like a peach about to burst?"

"Like a peach in a dumpster on a hot day."

"Gee, thanks for that. What every girl wants to hear."

"Blame the lumpy couch."

"Guest room's at the top of the stairs."

"Too tired to make the climb."

"I know that feeling."

"Take vitamins." He laced the boots.

"I take too much shit."

"I keep the pill people rich."

"We must share our memories."

"Which ones?"

"The pills."

"After the kidney and blood pressure stuff, the heartbeat stabilizer, the bone density stuff, the blood thinner and the coffee, my only memory is stomach upset."

"I get gas, too. What comes outta me is roses of spring."

"The thorns."

"Don't watch my ass. Might make you depressed."

She was out of the room before he answered.

Grace and Nick were at the kitchen table.

"Grace, I left the armor under the coffee table."

Jones sat next to the skillet.

"Anyone want refills?"

"No," they said.

"I got armor," Nick said.

"Is Mona eating?"

"She's into toast dry and coffee black." Grace cleared the soiled plates.

Jones spooned egg and bacon on one plate. Stacked griddle cakes on a second. Drowned them with warm maple syrup. Sprinkled pepper on the eggs.

"Not hungry?" Nick crumpled the empty cigarette pack.

Grace head gestured at the window. "Starting in again."

Light snow fell.

Nick opened a fresh deck.

"Build you a snowman, sheriff?" He pushed away from the table.

"A snow daughter."

"It'll shake out." Nick went for his jacket.

She poured the last of the coffee. "She's a worry I can't assuage."

The men looked at each other.

"Appeased is what I mean."

The men shrugged.

"Send me a postcard, Steve?"

"Yep."

He wiped his plate with a griddler. Washed down the cake with Coffee.

Nick came in, exhaling smoke, slapping gloved hands together.

"Colder than the Arctic Circle during a cold spell. I did my time in the Air Force, stationed in Iceland. Good name for it. Ice up the wazoo. Your heater work?"

"Last I flipped the switch." Steve stretched.

"I'm leaving my wheels here, Grace" Nick said.

She nodded.

Mona bounced in.

"Leaving already, Uncle Nick?"

"Business, dear."

"Too bad."

He patted her ass.

Under the nightshirt the round rear melons danced.

"Why, Uncle Nick." She kissed his nose.

"Smell sweeter than old ma." He cupped an asscheek, pressed a thumb against the solid meat.

"Nick, when you get back, your tires might be slashed," Grace said.

"Ouch."

He backed away, and into Jones.

The trucker fell against the table edge. Discs near the tail bone pinched.

"Dammit."

"Sorry, Jones."

Nick kissed Grace's forehead. Her breasts strained the halter top, filled his hands.

Mona gurgled. Steve looked away.

Grace squeezed Nick's groin. "Keep doing that and I'll lock the doors with you inside."

"Keep doin' that, and I'll need a change of jockeys."

He rubbed her back. She flattened against him.

"Save some for later." She pushed him away.

"We should be back in four days," he said. "Two days out. Two back. Sound right, Jones?"

"Depends on the roads."

"Interstate's salt and sanded into Wyoming," Grace said.

"The detours'll slow us down. Am I right, Steve?"

"Sure are, Nick."

"Helluva time of the year to go sightseeing." Mona poured a cup.

"Not much to see," Nick said.

"I've seen it all. Too many times." Jones massaged his lower back.

"Need anything?" Grace said.

"Besides you?" Gray said. "A thermos."

"Oh, right." Grace filled a five-gallon thermos. "Don't have styrofoam."

"Pick up a pack when we stop for smokes," Nice said, out the door.

The wind rattled the window curtains. They clicked against the panes. The chill hardened their nips. They shared a grin.

"Girls bein' girls," Mona said.

Steve hoisted himself into the cab.

"You move like a cripple." Nick slammed the passenger's door.

"My dancing days are done." He keyed the ignition.

"I used to be quite the man on the dance floor. Knew all the moves. Knew what the broads wanted, and gave it to 'em."

"Must've been a sight."

He pointed the rig at the road.

"Big as you are."

"I wasn't always fat. Nobody dared call me fat." His voice dropped to a lower register and stayed there. "One chump found out that not all fat men are jolly. Damned if he didn't curse himself for believing otherwise."

Jones turned onto a westbound four-lane access road.

"After we side-road it past the inspectors we'll pick up time on the interstate."

"When do we stop for coffin nails?" Nick coughed.

"Freemantle's ten miles farther on."

"I'm about to go Into nicotine withdrawal. You'd know if you smoked."

"I used to do a lot of things. I never smoked."

"What did you do?"

"Believed in family."

"I went from the orphanage to juvie hall to a military barracks to Harry's warehouse."

Jones grunted.

A blinking sign outside Freemantle announced Quick Gulp Smokes and more a half mile ahead.

In front of the store Nick tested the running board for ice.

Jones kept the motor running.

When Gray went in Jones floored the gas.

Mouth wide, Nick ran out, brought out the thirty-eight.

Before he got off a round, the deuce and a half cleared the drive. Oaks along both sides of the road provided cover.

THIRTEEN

A TWO STORY WHITE FRAME MANOR HOUSE with an open porch was the only house on the east-west four-lane.

Outside Freemantle ditches were glutted with scrub brush and wild trees seven to nine feet high. Squatters shacks were well to the south.

Jones left the rig in the front drive behind the van.

"Ready?" he said to the plump, middle aged woman who answered the door.

"All set." She squeezed his hand. "Got time for a cup?"

Karen West's younger sister, Babe Barnes and Babe's husband, Arnie sipped coffee at the kitchen table.

Ammo boxes were stacked on the counter, below the north window. Sawed-offs, AK-47s lay on their sides beneath the counter.

"Morning, boss." Arnie reached for the carafe.

"How's the big city?" Babe brushed her blonde bangs.

"Big."

Karen finished packing a large, brown paper sack.

"Coffee's strong enough to wake Woodrow Wilson." Jones set the half-empty cup on the linoleum covered table.

"Got enough hair on it?" Karen said.

"That's what she asked." Arnie squeezed Babe's thigh.

"Now, honey." She gave a short laugh: part embarrassment, part promise.

"Company's coming."

"How close?" Favoring his right leg, Arnie struggled out of the chair. "We can outrun him. If we leave now."

"There's a quicker way," Arnie said.

"Not if we don't have to." Steve headed for the door.

Like Jones they wore greatcoats, flannel shirts, jeans, boots.
Armor in hand they followed him out.
"Ride with you?" Karen said, outside.
He nodded.
Babe and Arnie took the van.
"Sandwiches and coffee." Karen hefted the brown paper sack.
"Pour me a cup?" He worked the ignition key. "For later."
He put a pill dispenser on the dashboard.
"What's the job?" she said.
"I remember you wanting to visit LA."
"One place I wanted to visit out there. What do we do once we get there?"
"We stop, I talk, we exit."
"Simple."
"You and yours will make it simple."
"In and out is how we like it."
After a mile, Karen said: "Should have brought harmonicas with silencers. So happy to see you I forgot."
"We won't need 'em."
"We never do." She grinned.
The road took them over a hillock, then down a one-lane cowpath.
Farther down on the interstate the weight station and truck stop were obscured by fog.
Jones dropped the clutch into granny low.
The van pulled alongside and Babe said: "I got to squat."
"Watch out for poison ivy," Karen said.
"Watch out for my daddy's lovin' arms." Babe giggled.
"Not his arms you need to worry about." Karen poured coffee.
"I'm along for protection," Arnie said behind Babe.
"You, darling, are the reason I'm warning her." She winked.
"Back in a flash with the gash." Arnie took Babe's arm.
They climbed the incline, into the copse above the cowpath.
Jones reached for the styrofoam cup.
He took two tabs from the dispenser.
"Calcium. Want a cap?"

"I get calcium from moo juice, cottage cheese, yogurt. My gas drives the young folks outta their bedroom."

"We're all friends here."

"There, too."

He swallowed, sipped, took another pill.

"Are you taking more stuff since last time?"

"This last one is Alendronate. Keeps my bone density dense."

"Losing bone marrow?"

"Going through the male-a-pause."

"Been down that rutted road. Bones intact."

A mile later:

"Want something more substantial than coffee?"

"Not when I'm on the wheel."

"A sandwich. My specialty."

"Peanut butter and Swiss cheese on rye."

"Makes a good girl laugh and sigh. Babe's rhyme from when she was going through her girlishness."

"Seems like . . ."

"Sure does."

"I miss your folks."

"Seems like they were here, doing the once in awhile 'jack' job with you, and then they were gone."

"Still hear from them?"

"Once, twice a month. A big hello from sunny Southern Florida. Ma phones. Dad's usually fishing from their dock. She and the old man sure wanted you to take over the jobs, the farm. That's all they talked about."

"You and yours are doing fine without me."

"We'd do better if we had you."

"I'm a freelancer with a truck now."

"Bert and Matilda West and son-in-law." She looked into his eyes.

Her perfume was everywhere.

"Did Arnie drive you out? You never said."

"Jacking is okay. Killing isn't."

"He thought your exit was because you were weak."

"I like freedom."

"Bessie's still up there over the dash."

"Is that so? Yep, you're right. I keep her oiled, loaded and next to the license to carry. I can use her if I have to. I wouldn't enjoy it."

Zipping his fly, buttoning her easy riders, Arnie and Babe came down the incline.

"It all came out just great," Arnie said.

He held the van door for his wife.

"Any treats left, darlin'?" Arnie said.

"Two." Karen handed him the sandwiches.

Babe rolled the window. "Coffee?"

"Yeah. That." Arnie held the sandwiches in one armpit.

He filled his hands with styrofoam.

"Honey?" Holding the cups, Arnie unwrapped a sandwich with his teeth. "That's your cue."

She scooted to the driver's side.

After Arnie positioned the cups on the dash, he reached behind him for a sawed-off.

"Just in case."

He tucked the shotgun in the space between seats.

"There's always plan B." Jones unwrapped a sandwich.

"What is that, boss?"

"Stay tuned."

"When we wing it I gotta sing it. " Arnie jabbered a line from that country novelty: *Chief Cherry Hill.*

Jones walked over to the van.

Leaning into the open window, he said: "What's behind us . . ."

"What's behind us?" Babe said.

"Nick Cray. From the Lance Group."

"Where, exactly?" Arnie's face was expressionless.

"Ten miles back."

"He must've got a flat," Babe said.

"He was on foot."

"Flat footed by now." Arnie glanced at the rearview mirror. "Don't see anyone."

"If he flagged a lift he'd be down there, lover." Babe shoulder gestured at the interstate below.

"Which means he could beat us to where we're going."
Arnie scowled. "I don't know everything but I do know this. If
you're being chased, you get there first."

"He has a cell. He has a friend in Arnholt." Jones headed for
the rig. "Add it up."

"Why didn't you add it up?"

Jones returned. "I didn't have the inclination."

"Incla-what?"

"It means . . ."

"Don't care what it means. I only have a GED so I don't
know all those fancy words. I do know this: you could've
dropped him with that twelve-gauge, left him for the
squirrels."

"Yeah, Arnie, and we could've graduated high school,"
Babe said.

"This is your paid vacation, kids," Jones said.

"I left my debit card at home. Damn."

"Do we keep the money?" Arnie said.

"Wire transfers."

"We won't see penny one."

Jones nodded.

"Then why are we going there?"

"To jack the goods before we unload."

"We detour the goods to a storage bay and deal from there.
Don't that make more sense?"

"We stop at their back door. They look. The look's all they
get."

They looked at Jones, at each other.

"There's a bonus for you and yours if this deal's clean."

"From who?"

"Me."

Arnie said: "Never told us what's back there."

"Stuff I don't understand and can't explain." Jones turned to
go. "The parts connected will make a Fourth of July display
look like cat's eyes in a foggy night. If what I hear is the
straight eight."

"Wait a bit now." Arnie walked Jones to the rig. "Me and
the Babe are angling for a babe and one of them costs more

than I make sweeping streets and growing shit and doing the once in awhile gig for you. So, if you're up to taking a smaller bite so she and me can have a larger mouthful, we'll name the first born: Steve Jones Barnes. Sound do-able?"

"We get this deal done. Then we talk."

"Fair enough."

Steve eased open the driver's door.

Karen woke up. "Oh. We ready to roll already? Do I have time to do a ladylike thing?"

"We do."

She took his arm, up the incline.

"This is so domestic." She dropped her jeans, pulled the thong below her knees.

"Sweetest ass this side of a Vegas bottoms up review." He unzipped.

"Easier to shack with." She tensed until the stream started.

"A force of nature. Your package."

"No forcing required. I'm always wet for you. I hoped, the folks hoped we'd find things in common besides jacking."

"Would've been nice." He directed the stream at an elm trunk.

"Never saw you void it out. Kind of nice, cozy. Like ma and pa at home, using the same facilities, at the same time. But, say, how come your water's coming out like that?"

"Like what?"

"Splayed. Like a duck's foot."

"Dunno."

"Hurt?"

"Why should it?"

"That childhood injury."

"What about it?"

"I just never noticed your flow."

"What's to notice?"

"Well, coming out like that has to hurt."

"Cramps once in awhile. It isn't like Old Faithful out there in Yellowstone, so don't wonder about it."

"I won't."

"I'm still a man."

"I know."

"That's all you need to know."

"I never thought of you as anything but." Her brows flew. "Hell, did you bring the A.W.?"

"T.P.?"

"The ass wipe."

"I didn't need it so I didn't bring it."

"Oh, well, what's a drip or three between friends?"

"Us? Or your thighs?" When she stood the belly roll covered the upper part of her mound. Thick brownish red hair curled along the smooth slope.

"Like what you see?" Her thighs tensed.

"Always do."

"Well?"

"The job's got my balls."

"Pencil you in for whenever?"

"When we get back home."

"Later then." She finger-combed her grayish red bangs.

Leaves, the color of corn flakes, deadened the approaching foot steps.

Babe came from behind a tree. "Your gentleman caller, boss, might be calling."

FOURTEEN

COMING DOWN THE INCLINE Grace's van slid in the gumbothick mud. A half mile away it negotiated the cowpath's ruts.

Arnie crouched between his van and the incline. The sawed off was steady. The butt rested on his knee. The muzzle, aimed at the approaching vehicle, did not waver.

Babe climbed on the van's hood, then onto the roof. She lay flat, aimed at the van. She did not shiver, or blink.

"There's an easier way." Steve and Karen climbed in.

"No easier way than this." Arnie focused with one eye.

"Another quarter mile." Babe bit her lip.

"Move the van."

Glaring, the couple broke formation. Thirty seconds later they were in their van.

Babe wheeled it around the rig and stopped in front of it.

Inreverse, the three-ton transport shimmied at Grace's van. She slid, backing down the access road. The road leveled off. He floored the gas. The rig hit the mid glutted pot holes and ruts. "Welcome to plan B, hon."

His lower plate and the few remaining teeth ground together.

Grace's van wallowed in gumbo.

The truck's rump slammed the van. Metal strips flew across the hood. She and Nick bailed. "The van's front end disappeared under the rig's tail.

He hit the brakes. Jerked the twelve-gauge from its mount above the dash. Grace lay on her side, facing him. She groped her hip holster. Before she had the sidearm aimed, Jones was out of the truck.

"Lay it on the ground. Now push it away. Stay down."

Gray lay on his side, cheek against the curb.

Arnie and Babe made their exit breathing hard, sweating, squinting.

"I'm liking plan B, boss."

"What do we do with 'em?" Babe swung the muzzle from Grace to Gray and back again.

Arnie said: "If I wasn't happily knot-tied, damn, I know what I'd do with all tits and ass all the time."

"Yeah, like you could do something grand." Babe spat.

"All men go through that every so often, dear."

"Stop whining. I still love ya."

"I sure hope you do."

"Gimme your cell."

After Steve phoned the highway patrol he got back in the truck. Gray stirred, moaned.

"Dammit, Jones. When Johnson finds out your ass will be impaled on barbed wire." Gray winced. "With the rest of your package."

With her toe, Babe nudged the sheriff.

"Get off me, bitch." Grace threw a fist, missed Babe's ankle.

"Don't talk to my wife like that." Arnie showed his sour face.

Nick groaned.

Arnie pocketed Gray's thirty-eight. Examined the cell phone, dropped it. From Gray's wallet Arnie took forty dollars in small bills but left the credit cards.

Gray shivered.

"Cold down there, pappy?" Arnie tossed the wallet in Gray's face. "Where I'd send ya it's hot all the time."

"About done?" Steve began the short walk to the truck.

Arnie was at his side. "Where's their arsenal?"

"In the van. Worth about a buck in a junk yard."

Arnie looked under the truck. "Guess you're right, boss."

Babe collected Grace's hand gun and ammo belt.

Sipping coffee Karen looked at two approaching specks.

"Getting company." She dropped the empty cup on the cab floor. "No DNA. No way."

"Don't worry about us ratting you out to the cops, Jones."
Nick flinched. "Where the highway ends that's where I'll be.
Waiting."

"Let me play my one-note violin, boss," Arnie said from the
van. "From here I won't miss."

Jones hoisted his weary weight into the cab. "Later. If we
have to."

The rig inched in reverse until the steel ball and the truck's
tail separated.

Arnie sang, off key: "California, here we come." Three days
later, after peanut butter and cheese and coffee and sleeping in
shifts on deserted back roads, Arnie sang: "California, here we
is."

FIFTEEN

THE SIGN AT THE BEVERLY HILLS ENTRANCE read: "No trucks over one ton."

"I know that," Steve said. "My brain's asleep."

"Like the rest of me." Karen covered a foul belch.

In the driveway of a convenience store, Steve U-turned. With the van dogging the rear end, the truck rumbled to a truck stop off the coast highway outside Santa Monica, came to a stop under two dying palm tress. He set the tracker and alarm.

"How soon does the watercress kiss the concrete?" Babe flopped on the double bed.

"We got some sleeping to do." Arnie dropped at her side.

"Another day won't piss off anyone," Steve said.

Karen pulled a hard-backed walnut-tinted chair to the foot of the bed. She sat hard. The dry wood squeaked.

"Ouch. Damn."

"TOFA." Steve dragged the other chair from its corner.

"What's that mean?" Arnie said.

"Tough on fat asses." Karen rubbed her left buttock.

"Don't you guys have a room?" Babe gave a wide-mouthed yawn.

Arnie tilted her head. "I can see your womanly place from here."

Babe pushed him away. "That's the only view you'll get. Till later." A yawn that showed the result of bad dentistry. "I need Zee time."

"When do we eat?" Arnie re-tied his left boot.

"The coffee shop looks clean," Steve said.

"How about Hamburger Hamlet?" Arnie tied the other boot. "Or Will Wrights?"

"How about the coffee shop?"

"Okay, boss," they said.

"What do we do till then?" Karen said.

"Six guesses." Babe fluffed the pillow. "Harder than a cement slab. Nothing's perfect."

She dropped her head. A moment later she snored.

Arnie smiled at her, at Steve and Karen. "When's the wake up call?"

"When we wake up." Steve shuffled to the door. Karen and Arnie followed him out.

The sun warmed their faces. The breeze was salt and oil heavy.

"Smells better than sow-shit back home," Arnie said.

Two deck chairs were on the patio at the end of the walk. Karen stretched out on one.

Across the drive, behind the privacy fence, at the wading pool, a woman ordered her child to be careful.

The child said: "Okay."

Arnie and Steve checked the van and the rig.

Arnie said: "I should've sent that pair to glory."

"Wasted armor."

"A pulled trigger prevents sudden surprises."

"Nick wants to be on the dock when we take the final boat ride."

"That's my point."

"We need to be one stroke faster. That's all."

"I'd be faster than a kid with his first sex thought."

"Which is why you're here."

"Where are they, I wonder?"

"Who knows?"

"Why aren't they doing the old boom-boom?"

"From a hospital bed?"

"He knows where the contact is?"

"I get there first. If he beats me there, you do what you do."

"I'm only as good as that first round."

"That's good enough."

Steve woke Karen.

Their room smelled of Lysol and Airwick.

Karen placed the safety chain.

"After smelling each other, this is a real thrill," she said.

"Who showers first?"

"Can't we share?"

"One of us has to stay out here."

"A PTA takes seconds."

"Puss, tits and ass isn't what I need." He bent back until the lower discs let him know when to stop.

They began to undress.

"I got the hot squats." She held him. Her breasts filled. The nipples hardened.

"Anything you can do for me?" Her hips rolled.

Her stomach rippled. Her goose-fleshed buttocks filled his hands. Her skin warmed.

They were sweating. Sighing. On the bed.

She tossed his shirt and undershirt.

He peeled the thong to her ankles. She kicked it across the room.

They lay in a humid embrace, kissing, nibbling, tongues flashing. She smelled of talc and sweat and pussy.

"Do me!" She lifted her pelvis.

Her head rolled. Eyelids fluttered.

His mouth covered her clit.

She yelped.

Tickling hairs, an overpowering wetness.

He tongue-thrashed the tiny gland.

She shrieked, pistoned, bucked.

"Oh . . .baby . . . please . . ."

She whimpered and squirmed.

He pinned her. He sawed her vagina almost to the ass crease.

Like a hitchhiker's thumb, his cock thrust. He shoved it in.

Her muscles sucked him in, accepted what he gave, closed on it. Her thighs abraded. Her heels pounded, tangled the sheets.

The few drops went in deep.

They frenched. She palmed the soggy, shrunken thumb.

She nibbled his ear, whispered: "Next time use my ass. Tighter. Hotter. Easier to manipulate those muscles. I'd love it if you could make me shout. Make me shit. Best enema there is: cum. I'd really love that. Any time soon?"

"No time soon."

"I can dream, can't I?"

"Set it to music."

"Already been set."

A pounding at the door.

"Chow time," Arnie said.

Karen gathered her clothes. "No time for a shower?"

"No time."

She pulled his penis. "Small but mighty."

He rubbed her clit. Her slow, husky laugh made Arnie blush.

"Geez, givin' me the hots."

"When aren't you hot?"

She squirmed away.

"I gotta see what the babe's doin'." He left.

Steve stepped into his jockeys.

She tossed his shirt and undershirt. "Remember my used to be?"

"Old man Ortha."

"Nearly blind, he was. Which is how he happened to be speeding down I-680 and right into the ass-end of a stalled oil tanker."

"I remember."

"They found pieces of him a year later. He taught me some foxy moves that you might enjoy. He was, well, deprived in the prick department. There are lots of moves guys with micro-meats can do to make it worth unzipping it. Although what you did was top of the list."

"Feel it at the top of your cunt?"

"Passed through Clit City. The boatman paddled for all he was worth."

"Just part of my neighborly service." He patted her rump.

"Make 'em dance, baby." She worked her pelvis.

"The tank's full." He pressed his groin against her buttocks. "The fuel line's blocked."

"Not even a dribble?" She tilted her head.

They kissed.

"Well, 'tanks' for that, anyway." She disengaged.

"Yeah, 'tanks' for the memory, like the song says."

From the other side of the door: "Hey, boss. We're ready. Are you still in there?"

"I was." Steve went to the door.

"We got our dinner boots on," Arnie said when the door opened.

"Polished and tied and ready for steppin' out." Babe stepped into the room. "This place could use some character."

"All the characters," Steve said, "are standing in the doorway."

He led the way out.

SIXTEEN

THE DINNER SPECIAL WAS PORK EYES. Two rolled pork slices embracing baked potato cubes in their skins, with brown gravy. The sides were shredded lettuce with thousand island dressing and a tomato slice and a radish and a watery potato soup. Hard crust rolls and oleo cubes and, for the ladies, hot tea with lemon and coffee for the men.

"A real banquet." Arnie was lip-deep in the salad.

They were at a window-side table. A few feet away were the half full lot, the patio and the wading pool. The same number of pickups and SUVs.

After the meal Steve borrowed the van.

"When you get back don't knock too hard. Me and mine'll be doin' some knockin' of our own."

"Just say anything." Babe lightly slapped the back of Arnie's head.

Karen focused on the water-spotted ceiling. "Do I have to sit these two?"

"I won't be long."

Arnie's leer was gone. "I should be with you."

"The contact isn't expecting anyone else. Anyone else would make him jumpy. Jumpy hands can be filled with armor. Just like that."

He snapped his fingers. The long nails deposited grime on the finger tips.

"Well, boss, you know where we are."

"On the way in, we passed that two story faded brick down by the ocean." Karen pointed.

"So?" they said.

"There's one site I wanna see, and that's it."

"What is it?" they said.

"Children's rehab center. Means something to me. How about you?"

"No," they said.

"Here's the ten second explanation."

Steve checked his watch. The married couple nuzzled.

"Remember *Carmen Jones?*"

"No."

"It was a movie. Came out in the early fifties. Dorothy Dandridge played the lead. A small role of a soldier in love with her was played by Joe Adams. He supported her like her best bra. At the time he hosted a show on KDAY, a twenty five thousand watt AM station on the second floor of the rehab center down there. I once thought I'd want a radio career. Dad and ma had other plans and radio was what I did not do. Before I let them re-direct me, I wrote a fan letter which was answered by the station's only full time employee, Walt DeSilva. He was the staff announcer. What he told me about nineteen fifties major market radio was this. The industry in the big cities was unionized. Engineers belonged to one guild. Announcers to AFTRA. American Federation of Television and Radio Artists. In the early and mid-fifties network block programming was still the popular format. Most AMs were affiliated with one of the four major networks from mid-morning to late night. Quiz shows. Soap operas. Dramas at night and comedies and music shows with live orchestras. No FMs then. A few unaffiliated stations filled with music. This was before Tod Storz and top forty music and news and great contests. Talk radio was limited to sales pitches on the border blasters. The two-hundred-fifty-thousand-watters across the Tex-mex border. According to Walt DeSilva all the DJs on Kay-Day were ad agency voice talent. The agencies bought the time. Hired the voice talent. So all the guys spinning the wax on Kay-Day's twenty-five-thousand-watts worked for the ad agencies, not the station. Union rags demanded the presence of a staff announcer to do the half hour FCC-mandated station IDs, and other duties as needed. DeSilva recorded sustaining unsponsored programs for the Sunday morning block. He also catalogued whatever the various labels sent to the station. Forty-fives and thirty-three and a thirds were replacing the seventy-eights. The photo he sent me was Kay-Day's all-star line up. I remember who they were and what shifts they worked. I also remember Joe Adams sponsor: Burgomeister Beer. Buy a Burgie was the slogan. A while later he sent me an air check of one of his commercials He had this big bass voice with a slight Jamaican accent. His enunciation was to die for. That smile in his voice made me damp."

Memory was like an inoperable tumor.

Steve started for the door.

She stopped him.

"Don't you wanna hear who did what and when?"

"I wouldn't miss it." He sat on the bed's edge.

"The log went like this: sign on at five AM. Spanish language with Mario Ray until nine. Nine to one was Chico Cessna. He spoke better English than my folks. He spun his records for Anglos and was sponsored by a furniture store. One to five was Jim Ameche time. I remembered that voice from the Mutual network's Jack Armstrong, All-American Boy. Also, he sounded like his brother: Don. His sponsor was a record label and a wholesale record mart. Five to eight was Chico Cessna doing a Spanish language program followed by Mario Ray with the same format until One AM sign off. Kept that photo and air check for years. When Ortha and me set up housekeeping the stuff got lost. Or something. The memory was strong as the memory of that first time I tasted cock. Seeing that building down there, well, I gotta stroll over there. Anybody wanna come with me?"

"I'd love to make you cum." Steve palmed the van keys.

"Already have, darlin'."

"I wanna sleep." Babe covered a yawn.

"Me, as well," Arnie said.

"I won't be long."

She walked him to the van.

"Keep an eye on those two."

"When I get back."

"I got back. One that hurts."

"I got pills for hot flashes and lower back discomfort."

He took a breath. "Jasmine. You? The night?"

"Kind of night that forces you to lower the car window."

She stood on her toes to accept his kiss.

Her mouth was damp, ripe.

"If I don't leave now, I won't leave."

"After this is over we will have our time together."

"You. Time. All I want."

"Bone doctors up the wah-zoo in Omaha."

"The med center's booked."

"Live with me, Steve. I can drive you when they're unbooked."

"When I finish this we will see what's left."

She fanny patted him. "Go. Do."

A brush of lips.

She about-faced, and faced the rehab center.

In the van he consulted the invoice.

He backed onto Santa Monica Boulevard.

He didn't look back.

SEVENTEEN

BABE WAS IN DEEP SLEEP.

Arnie eased off the bed.

He used the outside pay phone.

"Hey, asshole. Want the boodle Steve Jones trucked out here?"

"Who the hell is this?"

"Wake up, asshole. I'm the guy with the gun that boosted your wallet. The guy who remembered your cell phone number. Wanna do a deal with me? Or your boss in Omaha?"

"What's your deal?"

"I give you an address. I find the shipment. I get paid up front. Ten thousand. Then we never see each other again."

"Ten thousand? What? I'm the Oracle of Oakview?"

"I don't know nothin' about that spot on the road outside Omaha. I know what I need. What's fair. What you can raise on your way outta town. Which needs to be real soon. Jones is on the way to a meeting with his contact. The shipment's within spitting distance. I can touch the rig without reaching."

"Can you boost it?"

"To where?"

"Hell, I don't know! I'm not out there! Wherever that is."

"Keep your cell charged."

After he hung up, he strolled to the truck. It had been awhile since he hot-wired a deuce and a half.

He remembered how to do it.

EIGHTEEN

THE FOUR-STORY WHITE AND PALE GREEN STUCCO was on Shirley Place between Olympic and Pico, at the east end of Beverly Hills.

The contact lived in a first floor studio.

Shirley Place was quiet. Palm-lined. Artificial turf from the sidewalks to the entrances of the two story houses and four story apartment bulldings.

Jones rang the doorbell of number one-oh-one.

A tiny, elderly man in a soiled brown suit stood in the doorway.

"Well?" he had a smoker's voice.

He held between thumb and forefinger a partially smoked, well-chewed cigar. The balsawood mouth-piece was brown with tobacco juice.

"Mr. Dirk?"

"Who are you?"

"Steve Jones. From George Johnson."

"ID."

Steve showed his Nebraska driver's license.

Dirk flashed his New York State senior citizen's photo ID.

The single was furnished with used furniture, mismatched pieces from motel close out sales and thrift stores.

Magazines stacked on a table faced a false-walnut two shelf book case. A few paperbacks were arranged on the top shelf.

Some of the titles:

Hell Fire;

Wantons On Wheels;

Tuxedo Square Job;

Nothing Funny About An Old Man Laughing;

Welcome To Hellville;

Artist As Autist;

Strangers At The Dance;

Savage Highway.

"This ain't a library." Dirk, sighing, eased onto a recliner.

"They all are written by the same author."

"That's right. One of thousands of writers who are never forgotten because they were never known, never recognized, never accorded the perks of even a sliver of recognition and the few dollars the recognition would have generated. He's collectable now. I have every title he wrote on that shelf and in storage. This obscure shit will make me rich."

"The rich control the world."

"Could be they do. I won't ever be that rich." He snapped his fingers. "Invoice."

He scanned, nodded.

"Each box. Each crate. Opened."

"About that." Jones sat across the room, on the couch.

"Do I impress you as being stupid? No? That's right. I'm not. I'm a physicist. I know what each piece looks like." He reached for discount house Velcro-fastened loafers.

He took off his slippers. His toes were discolored, gnarled, swollen.

He lighted the cigar. "Now would be a good time."

"After you hear me out."

Scowling, Dirk groped for his slippers.

"After George Johnson gets his money, he steals what he sold."

"He already has. From someone." The scowl went away.

Dirk's vein-lined face remained impassive.

"That's what I hear."

"From whom did you hear?"

"George Johnson."

"He confides in his employees?"

"I can't say."

"Didn't you just say?"

"I'm his blood, not an employee."

That raised Dirk's eyebrows.

But he said: "Stealing from my country. Bad business."

"That's his plan."

Dirk pursed his lips. With the back of hand he rubbed his cheek. Two day's worth of whiskers scratched.

"What's in this for his son?" He blew a funnel of smoke at the ceiling.

"He mistreated my mother, my wife. Me."

"And, perhaps, you can cheat papa out of what we've paid."

"That would be a bonus."

"No bonus. Because we wired the money into a Swiss account. After we have the merchandize I wire the bank. A password is activated; the money transfers into one of his accounts. Mr. Johnson does not know the password. He fulfills his obligation, the money is his. That's all he knows right now. If he steals from us before the transfer he is right back at the beginning. He has the crates and boxes, and no money. He also gains the reputation of being what he is. So the boxes and crates might as well be filled with offal. Plus the annoying cold storage bills every month."

He coughed into a wrinkled, yellow washcloth.

"My buyers are no worse off than before. It would have been worthy of a Nobel prize in physics if we had been the first country to discover God's Particles. But we will accept that disappointment. Let another country win it. We will remain a country of ski slopes, discreet banks, and chocolate factories. Another worry for him. The U.S. lab that owned what is in those crates and boxes. When they discover your father's duplicity they will hang him by his testicles."

He leaned forward.

His lips were taut against saliva-ed teeth. The light in his eyes danced.

"Somewhere on the crates, if they are the original packing, will be stamped the lab's name or the manufacturer's name. Dump the merchandize on your father's doorstep. Contact the rightful owner first. Or deliver to the rightful owner. There must be a reward. Claim it."

He relit the cigar.

"When they came looking he would've dumped the stuff."

"Choices to consider. I relish them, have too few in my life. Youngsters have all the choices, it seems." He sighed, coughed. "Yes, they do."

Jones stood. "Don't get many visitors, do you?"

"Very few. Which is how I like it. Too many people, too many voices. Too many opinions can confuse an old man. Which, as you can see, I am."

"Confused?"

"Old."

"Ironic, isn't it? Johnson has wealth, the power that wealth buys, the obsequiousness that poorer classes have for the wealthy. He isn't content with what he has. Instead of scheming to fatten his purse he should be enjoying what he has."

The truck alarm went off.

NINETEEN

THE RIG RACED SOUTH AND EAST, along the Pacific Coast Highway. It passed through Torrance, slowed entering Long Beach, then headed for Huntington Beach.

The cut-off, a two-laner, emptied onto the highway a mile south of Long Beach.

The rig pierced the early evening fog. At the Huntington Beach interchange the rig slowed, then speeded up, passing the "Welcome to Laguna Beach" sign.

Faster through San Clemente's western edge, past Nixon's house of infamy—the estate that Nixon promised to give back; the sprawl paid for with taxpayer's money. When the former chief executive moved to Saddle River, New Jersey he sold the San Clemente property, at a profit, to a private party.

Jones kept four to seven car lengths behind the rig. When the truck slowed for through traffic Jones reached for a loaded AK-47.

Oceanside came and went.

Forty miles north of San Diego the truck veered onto a southwest eight-lane, skirted San Diego, lumbered through La Mesa, into El Cajon.

At the first industrial park advertising storage space, the jacker pulled in. The sign above the office door read: "Friendly Storage. We rent to amigos and anglos."

The fog pressed against the truck and the jacker. He went in, came out, papers in hand.

The pulse in Jones throat pounded. His back ached with relentless fury.

The jacker guided the rig to storage bay eleven. He lifted the bay's double doors. He drove in, got out, lowered and locked the doors.

He stretched, worked his shoulders. Jones was behind the storage bay. The van in the shadows.

The jacker tugged his crotch.

Jones nudged him.

"Uh, hello, boss." Voice trembled. Eyes wide.

"Hello, Arnie."

TWENTY

"AIN'T WHAT YOU THINK, STEVE."

"Tell me."

"Not much to it."

"All of it."

"I called Nick Gray. Told him I had the boodle. His for ten thousand. The deal was this: he drives here, inspects the cargo, pays off in cash. The lie is this: I help load his truck or van. He drives away, with me fatter in the wallet and him in sweet with Lance. The truth is this: I want him out here, cash in his pocket. He pays up. He gets the last rites. And burial under a tree somewhere. Besides the cash, I have the pleasure of icing the cake known as Nick Gray."

"Why?"

"Why the hell not! Me and Lance mix like sauerkraut juice and warm milk. Ten years ago I owed Lance. Couldn't pay. Got a visit from his number one who put a limp in the right leg."

"Took your time getting back."

"We didn't recognize each other. I wore a beard then. It wasn't until he was on his backside back there and I had his cell in my hand that I remembered him. I would've put him head first down a well only I know you hate bang-bang, and you was in a hurry to beat the highway law out here."

He rubbed his hands. "The boodle suckers him here. While he's busy looking it over . . ." He massaged his leg. "That's the last thing he sees. After I collect."

"Nothing in this racket's simple."

"I heard that."

"How far down the road?"

"Got to let him know where I am."
"Call him."

TWENTY-ONE

ACROSS THE TABLE, the women stared at each other.

"I don't wanna be a widow just yet," Babe said. "Not till the insurance is paid for."

"What do we do while we wait?"

"Wait," their men said. "It won't be long," Steve said.

Arnie said: "I-680 through Nebraska, Colorado and Arizona to California's like a hungry man's mouth. Wide open."

"Two days, ladies. If Gray leaves now."

"What if he brings back up?" Babe looked at the men.

"I told him no back up." Arnie, at the window, eyeballed their vehicles. "He agreed no back up."

"His word is like a rapist's promise."

"We'll find out damn soon," Arnie said.

Steve nodded.

He said to Karen: "How was your trip to radio ranch?"

"More like a stumble. The rehab center is an old folks day care. The second floor where Kay-Day was, is the Harry Stephen Keeler Memorial Library. Quirky mysteries, mostly by him with a few Ed Woods in the restricted section. Along the walls between book cases are photos of all those disc jockeys I mentioned." She jerked a chin hair. "Memories, like infants and old people don't travel well."

"Well," Steve eased off the hardwood chair.

Babe's yawn made him flinch.

"Trying to shout down a sequoia?" he said at the window.

"Just my way. " She finger-brushed her bangs.

"I figure he might have a contact out here." Arnie moved from the window.

"We separate them. Go from there," Steve said.

TWENTY-TWO

THEY PICKED THE ALTERNATE SITE. Kept alert in shifts. Kept in touch like people without cell minutes do.

Ten PM.

Outside storage bay eleven.

Karen and Steve were on watch. Smog itched their eyes.

From the van Arnie waved. Babe's cheeks filled with stomach gas.

"Sis likes a good belch."

"A good one is the high point of my day."

"Isn't being with me . . ."

"And that."

The wind off the pacific brought the dumped waste and dead fish stink. Steve turned up the greatcoat's collar. He thrust his hands in his pockets.

Across the yard a cat whined. Her eyes fog shrouded.

"Someone's missing her mate."

"I'm here."

She touched his sleeve. "Okay?"

He beckoned.

She snuffled. "Sinuses."

"Yep."

The cat yowled.

"Sounds like she found a mate."

"Those stump-prick moves Ortha taught you."

"I know enough to keep us grooving from now till next year."

"When this is over, hon."

Traffic hissed on wet pavement. Distant sirens. A vehicle with fatal-strength twin speakers assaulted whatever moved in the shadows.

"This waiting," she said. "Got me horny."

"Right urge. Wrong time." He checked his watch. "It's time."

Babe and Arnie met him at the front gate.

"Ready to rock," Arnie said.

"And roll. Over Mr. Gray," she snuggled against Arnie.

Karen met Steve at the bay. They crouched in the shadows.

Four minutes later Nick Gray's four wheel drive pulled in front of the van. Snow layers slid off the hood.

Arnie and Nick met in the space between vehicles. Their voices carried.

"The rig?"

"Not till money's changed wallets."

"I don't have it."

Scowling, Arnie turned away.

"Do you expect me to show with all that, without taking possession?"

Vehicles passed. None stopped.

"Get in," Arnie said.

Babe opened the side door.

"I remember you." Gray looked in.

"Nice to be remembered."

"What's the arsenal for?"

"We love company." Babe climbed in back.

Nick up front. Arnie drove.

Steve and Karen left through the back exit, crossed a gravel two-lane alley, through another gate and into another industrial park. The rig blocked the dumpster at the far end.

They took up positions behind a storage bay near the truck.

Five minutes later the van stopped near the truck.

The eight sentry lights turned night into day. Curiosity satisfied, a one-eyed Cheshire scampered behind storage bay ten.

Jones and Karen were twenty feet from their target.

Arnie opened the rig's double doors. He dropped the ramp. Nick went in. Arnie waited by the open doors. He patted thirty-eight's rib holster. He didn't look around.

Presently, Lance's enforcer came down the ramp, nodding.

"All there?" Arnie said.

"The right number of containers, sealed. That's all I was told to look for."

"Where's the small bills?"

"When I'm loaded and heading out."

"I'm not loading till the coins are mine."

"We have a problem."

"No, we don't." Arnie tossed the key ring. "The one that's taped is for the ignition. The other one's for the back end and front doors." Arnie drew the snub nose. "Or, I kill you now, and fuck the money."

"Tough fucking. Payday's aways from here."

"I got all night."

Arnie left the van in front of Friendly Storage's main gate.

"Where's your brains?" Nick said.

"That tall drink of water's been drunk. How's your personal life?"

When Gray's van pulled away into sparse traffic Karen waited thirty seconds.

Nick's van was at the intersection.

She slowed when Nick slowed.

"How's the back?"

"Better. Are you holding up okay?"

"Like my tits in a new bra. Where do you suppose?"

"A bank. Bus station locker. Any place."

"Carrying anything?"

"Never use."

"I could use a boost."

He rolled the window. The sharp ocean wind, wet as a mutt's tongue, licked his unshaven cheek.

She shivered. "That helps. Not much."

"The best I can do."

"The best I can expect."

"I expect so."

"A ho-hum kind of night."

"Careful, hon."

"Am I slurring and swerving? I can also sing a solid eight note octave."

"Save it."

"Anyone who hears me sing says the same."

Gray's van swerved into an outside lane, onto the freeway.

"Now it gets exciting." Jones sat up.

Gray nosed the van into an inside lane, nosed out a diesel, pulled back into the outside turning lane.

"He passed the diesel," Jones said to be saying something.

"Is that like passing a kidney stone?"

"Save the jokes for amateur night."

Gray left the freeway. The van bounced along a rutted four lane access road. Four farms. Two on either side.

Gray slowed. Then kicked it in high, flinging dust and mud clots.

"He knows," Steve said.

"He'd be blind not to." She lowered the high beams. Dropped into low gear.

He reached for a Russian AK. "We will see how much I remember from Fort Leonard Wood. The rifle range."

She bellowed. "Yah-hooo. Fort Lost In The Woods and Maggie's drawers. Damn me. I remember."

A two-lane macadam bisected an elm grove. Nick drove through it at eighty miles an hour.

No moon. Low fog. No breeze. The smeared reflection of the van's rear lights.

"If I squeeze a round I might hit the family." He leaned back in. "If I was better looking I'd be on camera somewhere, selling suppositories."

They came up fast on a dead end. Narrow one-lane paths left and right. A ditch straight ahead. One half mile from where they were to the ditch.

Gray slowed for the turn.

"Gimme that." She grabbed the Russian AK.

She braked, flung open the driver's door, used the door as a shield. She squeezed a round. The rear tire exploded. The van wobbled, fishtailed, swerved to the intersection. The four wheel drive slid sideways, tilted, toppled into the ditch. She charged at the tipped vehicle.

Holding the rifle butt against her hip, she aimed at the driver's door, "Out and empty-handed, Gray!"

The door opened. Dazed, coughing, Gray grubbled the fog.

Legs spread and braced, she stood at the ditch edge.

"I can irrigate your asshole from here. Don't challenge me."

Gray struggled over the sprung door. Dropping into the mud-filled ditch, he gasped, spat, lifted his head.

Jones came up behind her. "I'm going down."

Two hands appeared at the door.

He pulled out Arnie, then Babe.

"Wait a minute or three. I lost my peacekeeper." Arnie went back in.

"I lost my supper." Babe wiped her mouth.

Arnie smiled. "My dyed-blonde bombshell's always losing something."

He broke the snub-nosed police special. Snapped it shut.

He went over to Gray. The enforcer was semi-conscious. Annie's smile was gone.

"Don't die just yet. Don't spoil the mood."

Arnie stopped outside the splatter zone. He aimed for the husky man's forehead.

"The keys, bitch."

Nick glared.

"Pull 'em slow."

"Suckered me, cornbread."

"Gonna kill me, keep the cash. And the stash."

Jones dropped a hand on the thirty-eight. "Got the money?"

Arnie shook him off. "No."

"That's what this is all about."

"I dunno, boss."

Jones got between Arnie and the enforcer. "Where is it?"

"Will it buy my out-of-here?"

"Give it up. Aw-right, Arnie?"

Arnie thought, said: When I have the roll."

"In my pocket." He offed the cell, tossed it away.

Arnie aimed at Nick's throat. Karen aimed at Nick's belly.

Gray brought out his wallet, keys on a pocket clip, breath mints, pocket lint, one small, loose key. He held the key so they saw it.

"Sixty-eight-hundred block on Hollywood Boulevard. A mega bus depot. The lockers are on the first floor in back, near the crappers. Number four. The money's in a thick padded mailer."

He tried to climb out of the muck. Slipped. Slid back. His back smeared the van's mud clotted side bumper.

"Help me."

"Stay there," Jones said.

"If he blinks, I shoot," Karen said.

With thumb and forefinger, Babe formed a New York City style skin-kerchief. She blew a honker that frightened a nest of wrens on an elm's top branch.

"Not very ladylike, I know." She wiped on her jeans. "We're all friends here."

"More than friends." Arnie circled her waist, pulled her close, kissed her hard. "Damn, baby, you taste good."

"Puh-leeze. They might think we're in a breeding mood."

"I'm ready to do that knock-up thing any time."

"Scatter the loot on a cot built for two and I will screw you into the ground, smear girl juice all over them Franklins, Lincolns and Washingtons. Make 'em soggy as a whore's thong."

"Well, kids," Steve said. "I don't see any rescue units or eyes staring through lighted windows."

Steve went to the driver's door. Arnie began the short walk to the van.

Steve opened his hand. "I know Hollywood Boulevard, Arnie."

"Disneyland near there?"

"Not within forty miles."

"Hey." Babe measured her steps over the rutted ground. "Four boxes of super shells under the front seat."

"If we was out, where would we get any at this hour?"

Gray gave a sob and a snarl. "I'm freezing my bah-loo-kas over here and you're making with the chin music."

"Welcome to hellville, chump." Arnie flashed the finger.

"Back at ya, cornbread."

Jones grabbed Arnie's arm. "He's playing from a deck of jokers only he doesn't realize that. Not yet."

Glaring, grunting, Arnie climbed in.

He took out a pill dispenser.

"Need something for the go, boss?"

"Your snoring'll keep me going,"

"I don't do that. Babe's never bitched about it."

"She's a good wife."

"Yep."

"Mine was fine. If I brought home beans we ate beans."

"If I brought home beans we'd have a farting contest."

"Who'd win?"

"Babe. Although I can let 'em pretty good."

"Hearing's half the fun." He turned onto the freeway.

Arnie smiled.

The dashboard lights touched the one knee cap that was larger than its mate.

"We was on a veggies kick for awhile. One night she got the gun going for a minute. Maybe longer. If medals were given for extended asshole exits, she'd win one. Like one of them opera singers with the high notes that keeps the balcony awake. Vibrating like one of them forks guitar players use to tune their guitars. The aroma, coming outta my sweet puh-too-tee was like what comes outta a kitchen when a banquet's being created. Yessir, she's really talentedin that out-putting department."

"We all have some talent."

They approached the on ramp.

"I'd love her if she had no talent. If her gas was just ho-hum. If her body was thin as a finger, pointing through the fog. Or big as a hippo charging through the fog."

"You're preaching to the choir."

"Amen."

"Margo was like Babe. Not in the belching-farting aspect of our marriage. She took the final ride way too soon."

"I heard once on one of them girlie gas bag getogethers that it's better to love and then lose it than not having love at all."

"Bull droppings." Steve tightened his grip on the wheel.

"Okay, Steve?"

"Gas, I guess."

"You're among friends. All one of 'em." Arnie cut one.

Steve did likewise. "That'll do me till we get there."

Jones took shallow breaths. His underwear was drenched.

He rolled the window.

"Was it that bad? My gas?"

"My sweat. Too windy, let me know."

"The only wind is comin' down my poop chute. Here she comes." Arnie lifted his left asscheek. "There she goes."

"Babe isn't the only talented one."

"Why, thanks, boss." The pain worsened. At the shoulder, he braked.

"I need to get out. Drive?"

"Soon as you get back in."

He squatted behind the van.

A van, kicking up clots, shot past. It followed the road Steve and Arnie had just vacated.

"Busy nights for vans," Arnie said when Steve got back.

"For upset stomachs. And bung holes."

"Talking about chubby tummy in the ditch?"

"My exit wound. It's raw as a hooker's attitude."

"His will be, as well."

"I'm proud of you, partner."

"I suckered him good."

"What were keys to?"

"The house. The garage." Jones gave directions.

"Last usable thought was a new use for my left hand. I was twelve."

"I met mine when I was ten."

Traffic was sparse. He stayed below minimum speed.

At the northeast exit, he said: "Hang on, boss."

He cut in front of an SUV.

Steve's back pulsed.

"Great night for a drive, ain't it?"

"What I was thinking, Arnie."

Hollywood Boulevard's lights burned through the fog.

TWENTY-THREE

THE BUS DEPOT was east of Sid Grauman's Oriental Theater.

Arnie parked in the front lot, near the entrance.

Steve coughed on the smog.

Arnie said, after a look around: "More badges than bottles here."

Steve limped toward the restroom.

"Wait up, boss. I got to empty my toy soldier who shoots but never salutes."

Jones closed the stall door. Arnie used the urinal, zipped up, washed up.

Jones came out of the stall. "Everything come out okay?"

"If I was any lighter I'd bump my backside on the ceiling."

Over the loud speaker: "Bus departing gate four for Forrest Hills, Forman Gardens."

"A lotta fours." Arnie wiped his hands.

"I don't know any of those towns." Steve held his lower plate under the hot water tap. "Got any pain killers?"

"Nonprescription is all."

"Won't help." Jones put the denture where it belonged.

Two beefcakers in their forties, in uniforms, came in. "You two."

"Just a minute." Photo IDs dangled from their shirt pockets.

"IDs gents."

They showed their Cornhusker state drivers licenses.

"Okay, men."

"We were conducting a sweep."

"Not like conducting an orchestra." His partner winked.

Arnie faked a laugh.

"At these prices, guys."

"At this time of night, boys."

They went out.

"Not everyone can be Sammy Petrillo, fellas."

"Or Duke Mitchell."

The security specialist sang a lyric of that blues Ballad:

"Tricky Vicki was her name; had an act, wild or tame."

"She was the huntress after game." His partner was a tenor.

"In a bar, in a bar, in Toledo." The other one sang bass.

The ticket agent woke up.

They did a flash finish and a deep-waisted bow.

"We wouldn't waste time or talent if you fellers were bottle babes."

"Take your encore sitting down, sports." Arnie made a jaunty hand gesture.

"Do it on the quiet," Steve said.

"If you men need a lay-over there's a hotel around the corner and over a few blocks."

"On Highland."

"They rent rooms by the hour."

"Tell then Reed and Farrell said hi."

"Do we have to?" Arnie spotted locker number four.

"Why not?" Reed said.

"What'll that get us?" Steve said.

"One room."

"Two beds."

"And a double bolt."

"Or, you can stretch out on the bench over there."

"And take your chances."

"An epidemic of stolen shoe-itis, boys."

"Of course, for a fee, we can stick around."

"And do the act."

"I doubt they can afford us."

"Can you?"

"Can we what?" Arnie tugged his jockeys.

"Afford us," they said.

"Probably not." Steve winced.

"Well, then."

"We have a parking lot to patrol."

They went out the side exit.

"Shit, boss, what was that all about?"

"About too damn long." Arnie opened the locker.

"Here it is. Heavier than a new mother's tit."

Arnie pressed the envelope to his ribs. "I'm gonna love it when Babe sees this."

They waved at Reed and Farrell. The guards stopped harassing a rummy to wave back.

"I'll drive," Steve said. "You count."

"Me not a count. Me a king."

A block later, Arnie said: "Stop here."

They were on a side street under a sentry light.

"Duct tape," Arnie said. The brand that seals like cement."

Steve opened the door.

"Take one for me, boss."

A growling Doberman stopped Steve's stream. He crossed the street to another jasmine-covered fence.

Arnie howled.

The Doberman yelped.

TWENTY-FOUR

ARNIE SAT, DAZED, THE ENVELOPE IN HIS LAP.

Steve shook him.

"Shoot me now," said so softly Jones had trouble hearing.

Arnie's hands were filled with shredded paper, bubble wrap and two small stones.

"He even wrote a note, boss."

"Okay, Arnie, hold your water till we're gone from here."

They stopped in a stop-n-shop lot.

Arnie showed a stone. A hand printed note, taped to it, read: "Don't spend it all in one place."

"A real funny bitch." Arnie palmed a tear. "We know what comes next."

The smog lifted. On the access road their headlights showed a ditch. Steve pulled onto the dirt shelf above it.

Another set of lights showed up a mile away.

The moon's greasy reflection forced itself through the cloud cover.

Steve took two Russian AKs and ammo boxes.

"Load up, Arnold."

Arnie filled his pockets.

Crushed leaves under their boots sounded like burned toast being chewed.

The van, a mile away, blocked the road. Its headlights were directed at the shelf above the ditch and the wreckage in it.

Female whimpering stopped them.

Nick Gray was nude. He brandished a Russian AK.

Babe and Karen were nude.

Under their greatcoats Grace and Mona were nude.

Grace held a sawed-off.

"I gotta have the little bitch." Mona kissed Babe's forehead.

"No!" Babe slapped Mona's cheek.

"Little bitty bitch is feisty. I love feisty. Being the same size, we will fit together real well." Mona's voice skittered. "Feisty fuck."

Arnie aimed.

The slug punctured Nick Gray's throat. The impact threw him into the ditch, slammed him against the wreckage; capped molars shot across his lips.

He lay still against the twisted undercarriage.

The shot reverberated. A distant dog growled.

Grace wheeled. She squeezed a round into the shadows.

The echo rolled across the flat terrain.

They fired back.

Grace crumpled like a tin can in a vise.

Wild eyed, Mona threw her hands above her head. She grabbled air, growled.

Arnie held his wife, kissed her forehead. "There, there." He patted her ass. "Damn near daylight. We will be outta here before that happens."

The occasional spasm brought up another moan.

"That's okay, precious. Okay now."

Steve handed Karen's mud-spattered clothes. She shook them, put them on. The couple did not speak. Karen found Babe's clothes.

Mona picked up her garments.

Karen pulled them away. "Walk naked, tramp."

Mona leered. "Done that before." She turned to Jones. "Haven't I?"

"She doesn't feel the cold." He carried the armor.

Labored breathing rattled.

Karen took Steve's arm and a Russian AK. "We have to tell you something."

"Save it for Oprah," Arnie said.

"Oprah doesn't interview dead people."

"Doctor Phil does," Arnie said. "Save it for his gas bag get-together."

"Oh, wait. 'This is a Jerry Springer moment. " Babe looked up at her husband.

Karen said, as they walked: "In between grunts and groans, boys, sheriff bitch and her whelp admitted that she and hers were the first wave."

"Of what?" Steve massaged his lower back.

Mona howled. "Company's coming."

Arnie and the ass-shaker made eye contact. Mona winked. Shook her hips.

"Can't stop it, fools." With the back of her hand Mona wiped her nose.

Arnie goosed her with the rifle's muzzle.

"Oooohhhh . . ." She shrieked. "Oh, stop. Don't stop, you nasty smelly fuck."

Steve said: "Toss her threads. Someone will show up and give her a lift, in a car or on the hood."

Mona giggled, said: "Wherever you go someone will be sniffing your stink. When they find you, Stevie, there won't be any more stink. Except that final stink that soap and water can't wash away."

Her swollen irises glowed. She gave a DeNiro freeze-frame leer.

"Bitch dancer's right," Karen said.

"Be sure and tell big stud incorporated what we did to you and tiny tits. That'll flood their cocks."

Steve turned. "What's she tongue-shitting?"

Karen said: "Not now, baby."

"What we did when you were gone. " Mona shivered. "Makes me gush thinking about it."

"She can think?" they said.

TWENTY-FIVE

FROM THE VAN'S GLOVE COMPARTMENT Arnie took a flask.

"For emergencies." He took a sip before handing it to the women.

Mona sat outside the van. She waved her hands, yelled, made obscene hand gestures, and horror film faces.

"I vote to kill her," Arnie said.

"Pass out the dildos, boys." Babe coughed. "Kill her with kindness."

After the brandy cleared her throat, Karen said: "Omaha Harry Lance's crew's coming. 'The sheriff and the slut set up Lance's show."

"That's all of it?" Jones said.

Arnie keyed the ignition. "Ain't that enough?"

"Hey!" Mona stood in the headlights high beams.

"Grab her," Steve said.

"Why?" They said.

"I'd do it." An open-handed gesture.

"We can feed on her ass," Babe said. "If we get a hunger for moldy meat."

"The worthless piece deserved justice," Steve said. "Not a homeless mob."

Karen tossed her in back, under the muzzle of Babe's AK-47.

"If I get you alone, bitty bitch, I will make you dance naked for me. Make you love tongue and teeth, My fingers down your throat. In your ass."

Babe backhanded Mona.

"Do it again, bitty bitch!"

"What do we do when she comes down?" Karen said.

"This." Babe raised the rifle butt.

Eyes wide and wet, Mona watched it come down, within an inch of her jaw.

Babe pulled back. She showed Mona the AK's business end.

A quarter mile from the freeway two pickup trucks, straddling both sides of the road, came at them at full speed.

Arnie hit reverse.

Clods flew. Gravel pinged off the van's underside.

The van fish-tailed. Arnie got the van under control.

"Dammit! Gas is on empty."

They bailed at the first ditch they came to.

"Fire at flashes," Arnie said.

Mona was pulled from the van.

"Oh, oh, so cold. I'm so liking this." Her cunt gave off a sour, cock raising aroma.

With the AK Jones nudged her. "Get over there."

She stumbled, recovered, laughing.

"I so wanna fuck!" Her voice was shrill. "That fence post looks so seductive."

"Stay on the road. Walk!"

"Will you kill me if I don't?"

"Don't and we will see."

"That's right, screwhead." Babe threw a clod. It exploded when it hit Mona's back.

"Nasty Nelly! Why did I fall for a nasty broad?"

"Here they come!" Arnie said.

The ditch wall's jagged tree stumps, rocks and junk sloped twenty feet to the bottom. They followed Steve down.

The clouds broke. Splintered light showed a crumpled beer can, a soggy pizza carton, a whiskey fifth half filled with rain water, a gnawed chicken breast. Metallic stench teared their eyes, teased their throats.

From the road:

"Fleet's in!"

The truck doors flew open. Rifles and cocks in hand, the men leaped on her, dragged her to the first pickup, threw her on the blanket covered steel bed.

"They're down there!"

"No messing with the poon," a familiar voice shouted.

Harry Lance and ten enforcers.

"We're trapped," Arnie said.

"Not yet we're not."

A toppled, pocked, unpainted wood fence with a barbed wire crown leaned into a farm field, with a two-story house sprawled beyond the field.

They felt around, touched the wire, touched Jones.

He flattened a wire section.

They climbed over.

Lance's crew lined up above the ditch. They aimed into the darkness.

"Lights over here," one of the ten said.

A pickup straddled the shelf above. The heads went on.

Arnie fired twice; the lights died.

They spread out.

From behind a hundred-year-old oak, Arnie fired, fled before the first victim fell.

They fired at will, at once.

Shell casings flew. Slugs whined, gouged.

Men screamed.

"This is how we won the war, Arnie."

The men and Karen hit their targets; Babe pulverized a frightened jack rabbit.

Seven of Lance's crew, sprawled on the shelf above the ditch, stank.

The noise echoed, died.

The only sound came from a short distance.

Mona's guttural rasps kept the cadence.

The headlights showed the humping bodies.

Lance watched.

"Hurry it up. The other crew wants some of that."

The enforcer with his cock up her ass said: "They ain't making with the bang and boom."

"Probably finished them off." The cock being sucked was attached to a myopic buttonman. Short-sightedness gave him an arrogant look.

The cunt banger lifted his head. He looked between the butt fucker's legs.

"Uh, Mr. Lance?"

Lance stopped licking the thirty-eight's barrel.

"Not just yet, Harvey."

"Mr. Lance? Uh, uh, Mr. Bossman?"

His cock was trapped between scissored legs.

Arnie lined up the muzzle.

"No! Help!"

The Russian AK and the butt man discharged.

"Oh, shit." Mona smeared her titties. She was groggy; cushioned by drugs and lust, she licked her fingers.

The butt man's cannon fired a final volley.

"What-duh?" She half turned.

Number two lay, dripping, at her side.

She rolled, screaming.

Trapped, Harvey half-flipped. His cock popped. He fell on his back. He clawed the blanket.

Arnie put rounds in the myopic eyes.

Lance covered his face.

"What do we do?" Arnie said.

"I dunno. What *do* we do, Harry?"

Mona cowered in a corner. Her eyes and pussy lips were red rimmed.

"What do ya want, Stevie?"

"Is Johnson out here?"

"He's out there. In Arnholt."

Steve winced. "Your posse doesn't give a shit about toilet paper and clean jockeys. There's the cunt over there. There's you. There's the rest of us."

He paused.

The spasm passed.

"Yes?"

"Speak up, Harry."

"Yes!"

"What happens next depends on my partner here. How well you tell a story."

"What story?"

"Who else is showing up?"

"Open season on you, on what you're hauling."

"Are you on vacation? Working for a finder's fee?"

"Johnson told me to spread it loud. Why should some indy contractor get it?"

"He cheated the original buyer. He will cheat anyone who gets involved in this mess."

"We take chances every day and twice every night."

"Screw with me, Harry, and we will dance on your intestines."

"I get it."

"You will."

Humming, Mona massaged the cold cocks. She whispered each time one of them dribbled.

"Tiny e-john-u-lations. Cannot do me any good. Such well formed fuck sticks. Ummmm. if only there was some kinda life left."

She faced Harry.

"Mr. Omaha, you got any special deliveries for this empty mail pouch?"

She pried the pussy lips.

"Naw, I suddenly got dry balls."

"Suddenly?" Her laugh echoed. "Frog lookers like you got your cocks in your imaginations. Got nothin' between the legs except space. Born with your balls in your brains."

"She's yours, Harry."

"What am I supposed to do with it?" He stepped over and around the mess.

"Whatever you want." Harry climbed down.

"I'd be competing with every cock she ever sucked."

"Every cock waiting down the road," Arnie said.

"Hey, shits. It's my box yer babbling about. Where's my say in all this?"

"Stay with him."

"Or start walking." Arnie used a skin-kerchief to blow his nose.

"I showed them cunts of yours what they really are. Shitheads."

"I got a change of wardrobe," Harry said. "Yours, if ya want it."

"Then, what?"

"I drop you at a truck stop and that's it."

"My ma's sheriff of Arnholt County." She palmed tears.

"Was," Harry said. "Yesterday's law enforcer is less important than yesterday's lottery numbers. Ya wanna ride with the dead stuff?"

She jumped off.

Steve and Arnie were on their way to the van.

"First, you pull the offal off the back end."

"Awful offal? Hah! Made a joke."

"Shut up!"

"Well, where's the wet sponge?"

"Rent a shower stall."

"Where?"

"The squat and go. Next exit."

"How much?"

"Double sawbuck."

"How far is twenty dollars supposed to get me?"

"To Hell."

"You certainly know how to charm a squat-pisser."

Karen and Babe hunkered behind the van's open front doors.

"We thought you guys were walking home." Karen embraced Steve.

Arnie and his wife tongue-kissed, ass-stroked and hip-bucked.

"We got sixty seconds?" Babe said.

"And counting." Steve squinted at his watch.

Arms linked, he and Karen walked away.

Light penetrated the smog.

"Any stronger and we might be able to see each other," Karen said. She led him to a roadside stump.

He kissed a cheek bruise.

"Nick's gift?"

"I don't remember."

"I got the guilts."

"How'd it go at the bus station?"

"Like a hashish dream. A bad one."

"Figures."

"Sure does."

"Promise me. When you see Johnson talk nice."

"I have a plan for Johnson."

From the van came muted rhythmic grunts. The van's frame squeaked.

The steady up and down stopped.

"Play time's over." She stretched.

"No afterglow?"

"A swat on the ass, and a piss. That's romance in my crib."

The door opened.

"I got to drain my third leg."

Arnie pointed his stream into the ditch.

Mona and Harry boarded the pickup.

Harry avoided eye contact. Mona flashed the finger.

Harry drove toward the freeway.

"What happens with this stuff?" Karen gestured at the vehicles.

"Leave 'em."

"Did you leave DNA or prints?"

"We're safe."

Steve pounded the van doors.

Arnie appeared. "Already?"

"Got siphoning cans?"

"Lemme look. Hey, sweet cheeks, Any siphoning cans back there?"

"Two."

"Work, it, Arnie. My back doesn't have what it needs."

"What don't it have?"

"New discs."

"Like Freemantle's country AM radio station. No budget. Played the same damn discs over and over. The damn place finally burned down."

"By listener request," Babe said.

By first light they were veering around freeway traffic.

"We never saw Disneyland," Arnie said.

"We ain't gonna see it now." Babe snuggled.

He drove with one arm around her shoulders.

At storage bay eleven, Karen said: "Let me drive."

Karen opened the truck.

"I'm the one with the over the road papers," Steve said.

"Meet you where?" Arnie said.

"We can make it to Kingman on what we have," Babe said.

"Can you last it, boss?"

"If I can't you'll know it."

Steve paid the storage bill. By nine AM they were at the Arizona border.

TWENTY-SIX

AN HOUR EARLIER, Harry bought breakfast.

Over ham and eggs Mona cute-eyed two middle aged biker butchs.

The pair nudged each other. One whispered. They laughed.

"Found some friends already." Harry paid the check.

"They look dangerous. I love dangerous." Mona sipped coffee. "Here's your hat, Mr. Omaha. What's your hurry, Harry?"

"If you ever get to Omaha, keep going."

"That's aw-right, frog. Say what you mean."

"That's what I mean."

The door closed behind him.

The bikers came over.

Mona sat between them., grinning, trying for her most convincing shy eye-take.

"Hi-yah, fellas." She eyeballed the leather vests, cleavage, the breeches tight as a horny lover's hands lifting their buttocks. The knee-high boots.

"Hello, amateur," one breathed.

Mona leered. "Been waitin' for ya."

"We do like 'em young and inexperienced," the other said.

"Ever been gang fucked?"

"By two hot riders?"

"No, no," Mona said in a high, thin voice. "Please, ladies."

"We ain't ladies."

"We sure will please."

"Whether you want it or not."

"After awhile, you will want it."

They took her hands.

"Dearly want it."

"I'm dirty." Mona lifted an arm. "Smell, if you don't mind a nose bleed."

"Don't need to strain yourself. Does she, Maudette?"

"All you got to lift, girlie, is your twat when we wanna get in. Right, Claudette?"

"But, dykes and a half. I need to freshen up."

"We do that."

"All you got to do is be there."

"Oooohhhh." Mona dropped hands on their lower stomachs. "Feels so hot and curly down there. And I love your names."

"Love more'n that when we be done doin' it."

"I'm so wet." Mona shook like she was on lithium. "I'm drowning the crabs."

"We is clean, gash."

Mona nodded. "Sure. Like I am."

"We play discovery together."

"We got crab killer."

"Extra large jugs."

"Just like we is."

"Strong like we is."

"Only it won't give ya nose bleeds."

"We best be goin'."

"While the mood is hot on us."

They stumbled, laughing, for the door. They cupped Mona's titties. Slapped her ass.

The counterman said: "No rowdy crapola or I'll run ya into the next county."

"He's got two buddies. Cops, they is."

"We slice and dice you, and discount price you afore your pals finish their coffee."

"And shit their donuts."

"Yeah? Well . . ."

Their hogs angled in the spaces in front of cabin forty-four. Crossing the lot they frenched Mona; the petite blonde trembled, babbled pretend-shit.

"Oh, oh, I'm just gushing, filling my thong with sweat and suck juice. Oh, you nasty bitchs."

Maudette hoisted her in her muscular arms.

Claudette unlocked the door.

Maudette dropped Mona on the floor.

"Ow. Breakin' the merchandize before ya got it unwrapped?" She rubbed her ass. "Ouch. That ain't a good ouch, bimbette."

"Be patient, puss."

"We rub that."

The bikers frenched while they undid the leather vests.

Maudette's forty-four Ds dropped, slapped.

"After all these years." Tit against tit.

Claudette's were cork-tipped, crimson.

Maudette's nips were pink. They blushed when they brushed Claudette's bigger rack.

They grunted. Lip-chewed. Short, bursting inhaling, exhaling.

Their pelvises jerked.

"Uh, uh."

They licked saliva from each other's lips.

Mona was on her feet. "Shit, girls, you forgot me."

"Dis is the warm up, bitch."

"We gonna do the pitch right now."

They kicked off their boots, slithered out of their breeches, jerked their dark blue thongs, kicked the thongs at Mona.

"Bury me." She buried her nose and mouth in damp, inhaling the sweat, leather and screw juice smells.

She chewed, growled, eyes glinting.

"Maudette, we got ourselves a real prime piece."

"Well done, and sizzling to do it, Claudie."

They stripped the dancer, carried her, laughing, squirming, into the shower stall. Claudette cranked the water full force.

"Wow!" Nipple-raising cold coursed over their goose-fleshed sagging breasts and stomachs.

Yelping, the bikers high fived.

"Aaaahhhh." Mona's head rolled.

Spasms in her shoulders lifted her breasts, shook her stomach, thighs, asscheeks. Her vagina's sourness mingled with the bikers' sweat.

Claudette wielded a long-handled, stiff-bristled brush. She brought it down hard against Mona's ass. Mona recoiled, braced her palms against the sweating wall tiles.

Claudette rubbed her supple ass scarlet.

Yowling, Mona danced in place.

"How you like us now?"

"Yow!"

"She like us."

"She will like us better."

"Be gentle now."

Claudette hung the brush on the wall hook. She soaped a coarse washcloth.

"I see we got us a breeder."

"What she breedin'?"

"Gimme that crab killer."

She soaked another cloth with the acrid liquid. The syrup-like substance raised irritating fumes. Their eyes watered. Mona quivered; the oil slickened her mound. White dots fell from the stubble into the drain.

"Soap her good."

"Jus like we should."

"Ugh, oh, I gotta puke. It burns!" Mona's hips whipped.

Claudette massaged Mona's upper back. "Belch for baby."

"No, I can't."

"Stop yer whimperin'. Start yer belchin', girl."

"Or we paddle that sweet tight ass."

"Won't treat it kind."

"Cot me outta my mind."

"Tie yer titties in a bind."

"If we be cops we'd arrest you for being unclean."

"Oh, girls, if you only knew."

"Knew what?" they said.

"How ya got my crank shaft, goin' fore and aft."

Mona's voice voice was drowned by the water.

It flooded her cleavage, splattered the wall.

"We gonna have ourselves a party, pretty piece."

"One you ain't ever gonna forget."

"We get done with you, pussy, you ain't ever gonna go back to cock."

Eyelids clenched, Mona spread. Purring sounds from slack lips told the bikers what they wanted to hear.

"We bathe you so you be fit to fuck."

While the lukewarm water spilled over her shoulders her breath burst, eyelids fluttered.

"Yeah, pretty piece, you damn well better learn to love it."

"If yer gonna ride with us."

They jerked her away from the wall.

"Bend over!"

Mona did what was demanded.

She winced, eyes wide, gasped when the oiled finger went in, choked as the finger wiggled, spread the crab killer. The puckered hole popped when the finger came out.

The other biker fingered the blushing cunt crease.

Mona's knees buckled.

They caught her, held her while they explored her asshole, her pussy.

"Ugh." Mona threw her head into the spray.

The bikers massaged both holes.

"Yum, she is some snug pretty-puss. A real plum."

"We make her cum."

"As many times as she been some big stud's punch pillow and she's still tight as a schoolboy's fist."

"We gotta use a breeder's stick on them fuck tunnels."

"Make her jump and shout."

"Blow her mind out."

"I can't stand it." Mona ran the words together.

She sagged.

"Don't you sit on it."

"We wanna taste yer shit chute."

"Your cunny fruit."

"Your tittie beauts."

"Make you our hon."

"Make you get your gun."

"In the shade."

"In the sun."

"You be our punchin' luncheon fun."

"Low cal."

"Our gal."

"Your gal pal."

"We so good, Claudie, we gave me a cum and git it."

"Um, gotta have these." Claudette hefted Mona's small spheres, kissed the tips, washed them.

Mona's groans intensified.

"Hush, darlin'."

She soaped the cleavage, dragged the cloth to Mona's belly.

"Yessss."

Each touch, each pressed pressure point, Mona yelped.

Strong, callused hands squeezing forced plaster-cracking screams.

"Yessss, do me like you do me. Oh, yessss, oh, it feels so good."

"Ah, look how them hips carry on."

Maudette slapped the blonde's buttocks. A red palm print erupted on the dancing muscles.

"Look, Maudie, how big them boobies is gettin'."

"I loves big boobies."

Claudette dug her fingers into the heaving butt meat.

"Look-eeee how them boobies dance."

"They loves to dance." Maudette kissed Mona's throat.

Claudette tongued the clenched ass slit.

Mona's screams: unbroken, piglike.

"Open real wide. Lemme see that blind eye. Lemme taste the drool."

"Stop! Stop!"

"We is making baby here all bothered and blazing."

"Bitch's hurting me, also. So nasty." She smothered Mona with cleavage; muffled her cries.

"Make her lick them titties of yours." She hefted the ass meat, spread them wide, blew into the crease.

Mona yelped, swiveled, bucked, squirmed and thrashed.

"Blonde goddess."

"Our goddess."

"Captured."

"Wanting the rape."

"Where's that brush?"

"What you gonna do, girl friend?"

"Oil the handle. Shove it way in deep. She screams and we love her for it. She loves us for it."

Mona tensed. Her shriek rattled the exposed pipes.

"We loves ya, bitty babe!"

Their stomachs rippled. Their tits strained.

They kissed her lips, her breasts. They held her hips while they tongued her cunt and asshole.

"Keep you in chains, girl."

"Let you loose when we need girlie fuckin'."

"We feed you good."

"Keep you so clean yer skin'll squeak."

Mona's howl covered the sound of the door opening, the rapid footfalls into the bathroom.

"Aw-right!"

The two cops brandished sidearms.

"Party's over."

"I warned ya," the counterman said.

"Myron, get out."

"Police business," the other cop said.

TWENTY-SEVEN

TEN MINUTES LATER, the biker babes were dressed, handcuffed and in the squad car. Mona was wrapped in a blanket, still stuttering her statement.

"And then they forced me in here, stripped me and I couldn't escape," she said with the proper controlled hysteria.

"Were they terribly rough?"

"Have you ever been bathed by two high school drop outs?"

The cops exchanged winks.

"Well, you seem okay."

"I'm just okay, officers." She shivered, for show.

"I'm Pete Farrell. He's Jack Reed. Have you seen our act?"

"Where would that be?"

"The Down and Up Club on Gower."

"The Deep Well over on Highland."

"And a few parties."

"I'm not from here."

"We do songs, one liners."

"The whole hall of beans."

"Like this."

"The other day I took my feet for a walk."

"This baby in diaper she wanted to talk."

"I stayed, and listened long as I could."

"About her ride to this neighborhood."

"Sorry, officers. I got all kinds of aches. I don't think I'd appreciate your act."

They shut their notepads.

"We need to know."

"Fast or slow.

"Are you pressing charges?"

"No? Then on with the show."

"Don't want to press anything. I got to get back home. Can't wait for a court date."

Myron came in. "Fellers, your cargo's kicking the crap out of your cruiser."

"They try that sometimes."

"End up with broken toes."

Farrell and Reed started out.

"I really hated to bother you guys," Myron said.

"No bother."

"I clean up after them. Disinfect everything. I handle complaints. When it gets wild. Like now. A traveling man next door bitched about the noise."

"Pissed because he wasn't invited."

Myron shrugged.

The cops turned back, into the room.

"Miss, if you don't want to confront them we can drive them down the road."

"Dump them on the freeway. Make them hike back for their bikes."

"I want to confront them."

"Either one can flatten you with one well placed punch."

"I was born wearing track shoes. I can outrun anything on two legs and two wheels." She dropped the towel.

Their eyes widened. Her pussy lips blushed. The blush surged upward igniting fires in her eyes.

"See anything you like, boys?"

"Lots to like."

"Not on taxpayer time."

"Cross-country bus stops here every two, three hours." Myron's nose leaked, "Use the room till then."

"We can drop you at the super depot on Hollywood Boulevard."

"Less likely to get gang-shagged there."

"We do off-duty security there. We'd keep an eye out for trouble."

"Thanks. But, no."

"Your choice."

"Unless they destroyed our bus we have to let them go."

"Unless you changed your mind."

"Unless you want to press charges."

They looked at Myron.

"They paid for two nights. They got their two nights. The room looks intact, except for the soap which they used or stole."

"So you can't file anything."

"Guys, give them my room number. I get this need sometimes."

"They'd do more than paddle your posterior."

"Say, partner, that might make a great song."

"If we gig an S-and-M convention."

Before their exit they took another look at Mona. She turned, tilted her ass-cheeks, rubbed and slapped them. They jiggled, softly sighed.

Sighing, forehead veins dancing, the pair went out.

"Wonder what the wife's doing?" one of the cops said.

Myron stopped in the doorway.

"The invite's still open, miss. Whatever you need for the road."

"I can handle the freight. Noting to go back to, except a piss-ant of a gig and a house with a mortgage and some pasties and thongs. Boring shit I can live without. People I can live without." She looked at her thong. "Time for new contacts. Ride new things."

"Well, have a safe journey."

"Truckers go by here?"

"Sometimes they stop."

"Might get a lift."

"On his cock."

"On her tongue. I love choices."

"Out here not many choices for a forty-year-old chump change counter-jockey, writing his first novel, wallowing in depression of a first draft."

"Writing is for old men who can't fuck, and have endless time for a short time. Then it's the whirlwind of nothing for eternity. Amateurs in a game where the pros survive. And not many do."

"Gee, lady, thanks for the pep talk. Or was that poop talk?"

"Call it what you want. It's still a free country."

"Nothing's free. I got the tax bills to prove it."

"Where I come from you don't get to keep your coins."

"Foreign country?"

"This country."

Suddenly, all of Myron, except for his prick, stiffened.

Arms flailing, he sneezed. Nearby, a car alarm went off.

"Damn glad it wasn't a fart," she said.

"First, the snee . . . zing. Then the cough . . . ing."

"Coffee?"

"Coughing!"

Jumping as though manipulated by Merc Cunningham, Myron coughed. Regained control.

He drenched a dime store washcloth with nasal debris. He stuffed the rag in his back pocket.

"I can feel the wet," he said.

"That's what the last Johnnie I lap danced said." She was dressed. "See you sometime."

Giving her a hot eye of sex and need, the sort of look lonely men have given women since the discovery of companionship and its absence, he stepped away from the door.

The sidewalk was blocked by the two bikers.

They weren't smiling.

"Well, hello, girlie-gir."

"Goin' our way?"

She thought fast.

"I didn't file charges. You owe me."

"We love to own you."

"Only." An open-handed gesture. "What would we own?"

"File charges." A shrug that made her tits move.

"We been chased before."

"Still ain't been caught."

"We is the wind."

"Where I'm from we call that farts."

"We been doin' them since before you got the monthlies."

"Girls, you two are so off the shoulder." A forced laugh.

"Off the what?"

"Shoulder? Whose?"

"Figure of speech."

"Some figure." Wet-eyed looks.

"Some speech."

"More mouth than leg."

"Nobody's perfect."

"Bitty one, those charges? You can file."

"We still ride in style."

"Loved my leg in there."

"We love ya now."

"A cuff-taste kindles the cunt."

"We gets weary bein' on top all the time."

"We likes it when we get shackled and cussed at and handled like we was freight on a dock."

Myron came out from behind a dumpster.

"Fantasy can lead to a sad wake up. Or a happy make up."

"Who invited him?"

"Girls only, stud."

"If you ain't got a pussy in them jockeys you best do the walk-away.

"Drop anchor another day."

"In another bay."

"The only way."

"I can call the law," he said to Mona.

"Don't you dare!"

"Okay."

"Gals, give the okay or I go away."

The bikers exchanged nods.

"Well?"

"Wellll . . ."

"Promise you will take care of me."

"Sure, bimbette."

"We promise anything."

"We produce movies."

"We know how to make a promise."

"Movies?" Mona and Myron said.

"Do you need . . ."

"Nothin' from you, counter boy."

"From her? Ummmm. Now that's a script with a sweet ending."

"Sweet end is what she's about."

"Ass cuter than a pig snout."

"From way down Sout'."

"Bitty? Can you act?"

Mona said: "That's a fact."

Myron began a reply.

"We ain't jivin' at you, freak out party."

"Go back to your pots and pans."

"Your chickens and lambs."

"The ham what am."

"Pancakes with jam."

"Beef so raw it says: I am.."

"Chili with the bing bing."

"The spam with the bam bam."

Wailing, Myron covered his ears.

"Doggerel, doggerel."

He ran to the coffee shop.

"What's his problem?"

"He's a stand and deliver pisser. What ain't his problem?"

"I gotta tell ya," Mona said.

"Tell us?"

"What?"

"My career in your films'll be short."

"We always need talent."

"We wears 'em out."

"Four years."

"Max."

"After four, customers lose interest."

"We got a constant need."

"In the studio."

"In our rack."

"Iraq?"

"Hell no!"

"When did this get to be political?"

"Our best customers are over there."

"And we ain't talkin' about our soldiers."

"We talkin' 'bout Saddam, hisself."

"He was one."

"Needed girl on girl fun."

"And all-uh them that needs this need."

"To watch girls lovin' each other."

"Chemical Ali say they make him pee."

"Launched his boat clear out to sea."

"Them broads and studs do more than sip coffee and smoke water pipes."

"We got water for their pipes."

A shared laugh. Then:

"Bitty tits, you be international in a big way."

"In no time."

"Great. I really need the audience."

"She says it like she don't give a pimp's high pillow for our contract."

"I have this need."

"We don't?"

"Medicine's what I need."

"We got meth makers by the yard."

"In our yard."

"Don't need meth. And, yes, I do not have a lisp."

"Don't tell us you pee-gee?"

"Okay. I won't."

"Ain't what Maudette means."

"I'm not pee-gee. Worse."

"Can't be worse bein' knocked and locked into bein' rocked.

"Around the clock."

"I'm not gonna be around for four."

"Four is the outside."

"They burn out a-for that."

"We pays 'em off."

"We get holiday cards every year."

"Jus' visited one of our exes."

"Had us a whee of a time. Now didn't we, Claudie?"

"We did. A fact."

"Put me in a snuff film. Do me a favor."

"We don't snuff."

"Don't do that stuff."
Jus' real time fuckin'."
"Lotsa huff and puff."
"If that ain't enough."
"These gals talk rough."
"Low voice."
"Gruff."
"Makes their titties get hard."
"Dampen their muff."
"On the bed."
"On the cuff."
"In the cunt."
"In the duff."
"Films open in the buff."
"Don't waste time gettin' there."
"Mouth kissin'."
"Then in the hair."
"They talk real straight."
"We lets 'em swear."
"Fuck 'em here."
"Fuck 'em there."
"On the bed."
"On the chair."
"They do ass-tonguin'."
"We don't care."
"Got to put it."
"Somewhere."
"So why not there."
"And there."
And there."
"Bitty, when ya wanna leave."
"Tug our sleeve."
"You will be missed."
"We won't grieve."
"Lotsa poon on the way."
"Pick what we need."
"Any old day."
"Be our bitch."

"Till yer not."

"Wave goodbye."

"And thanks a lot."

"I never rode a hog."

"We will show ya how."

"Helmet first."

"Or we get caught."

"Hold on tight."

"Like a bargain just bought."

"With two victors."

"Of film wars fought."

"Fart if ya want."

"Just don't yawn."

"Swallow the dust?"

"Cough till dawn."

"Belch and sneeze."

"Then the cough is gone."

"So, bitty bitch, climb right on."

"Heaven's ahead."

"Then it's Forest Lawn."

"We will ride you hard."

"Love ya good."

"Bury you deep."

"In a peaceful hood."

"One day soon tell us why."

"When you be goin'."

"Straight up to the sky."

"Or down below."

"Wherever it is."

"We all goes there."

"When we leave show biz."

"Don't need to know," Mona said. "Not just yet."

"Will you tell us?"

"Dam well bet."

"We got a short ride. To our movie set."

"To Hollywood Boulevard."

"To a one-story ranch."

"With a big back yard."

"A shed's back there."
"That's where we works."
"Where we make them films."
"For the Arabs."
"And the Turks."
"Make them for girlie girls."
"Just like you."
"For old Lezzies."
"And Lezzies who are new."
"We love the work."
"They love the product."
"Lots of offers."
"Hey, how about it?"
"We make the film."
"We do the work."
"Doin' the work."
"Is a natural perk."
"Got me interested. Got me wet."
"Don't blow off."
"At least not yet."
"Before the cameras roll."
"We check you out."
"Body and soul."
"To see what yer about."
"Since you only hint."
"At what's the matter."
"We gets an MD."
"She see if you gets fatter."
"We don't know nothin' about birthin' babies."
"Makin' 'em belch."
"And we don't mean maybe."
"Belchin' them babies."
"Diapers, too."
"Ain't for us."
"Ain't for you."
"You be one of us."
"That's fer real."
"Don't make a fuss."

"When she cops a feel."
"Jus' slip yer feet in that steel."
"Let her do the deal."
"She tilts the table."
"For a look-see in."
"See straight up."
"To yer double chin."
"Up and down."
"To yer vertical grin."
"We find out what's go in' on."
"What makes you laugh."
"Makes you yawn."
"Keep this shrimp."
"From becoming a prawn."
"Make you a queen."
"Not a pawn."
"Can you cut it?"
"Long as I'm able.
"Fuck them standing.
"On a table."
"Fuck them in bed."
"Fuck them good."
"Hear me howl."
"Understood?"
"We wants throbbing clits."
"Asses that's heavin'."
"Womens that's dedicated."
"Into believin'."
"Cunts that's got perfume."
"In the shed."
"In our room."
"Sunday in the park with Jenny." Mona tucked her ears in the helmet.
"Jenny?"
"My first."
"Was she loving?"
"It was hurry up. Hide from it. In the showers next day she made fun of me. She enjoyed it much as I did."

"We was behind a plow when we was saved."

"Tornado tore the farm off'n the planet."

"Tossed our parents up a tree."

"Never found where that tree was."

"We been back and forthing it ever since."

"Miss givin' the folks a decent burial."

"Can't have everything."

They straddled their hogs.

"Come on, girlie."

They kicked the kick stands.

"Comin"?"

"Can't wait."

Mona mounted Maudette's cycle.

Myron said to himself: "There they go. Wantons on wheels."

Mona wondered how long before they found out about the AIDS, and what they would do when they found out.

TWENTY-EIGHT

TWO DAYS AFTER MONA BEGAN LIVING LARGE in that red-roofed ranch house off Hollywood Boulevard, Steve Jones paid for one night in a motel in Kingman, Arizona, near the expressway.

Six AM with a sharp, steady wind.

Storm clouds massed.

"A shower and a nap," Babe said, unlocking room number eight.

"I have plans, too," Arnie said. "Taking a nap's not one of them."

"That leaves us, Steve." Karen opened room number seven and went in. "Give me five to scope for bedbugs."

"Happy hunting," they said.

Steve was bent like the top half of a question mark.

"Arthritis again?" Arnie said at the van.

"Never left." Steve forced the straightening exercises.

"Surgery?" Arnie made sure the weapons were anchored to the wall box.

"Probably."

"Got a little left in the flask, Steve."

"Thanks."

"Save the thanks. It's convenience store brandy. Two thirds lighter fluid."

Arnie rummaged in the glove compartment.

"Here she is."

Steve took a swallow. After coughing, he capped the flask.

"Keep it for later, Arnie?"

"Forever, if you want to. I use it for snake bite."

Karen's eyes opened.

"Drink?"

She took the flask.

"I love nightcaps. Even at dawn."

"Rub my back?"

"Strip."

She straddled him, stroked the discs.

He held his breath. Exhaled when she finished.

"Better?"

"Yep." He got up.

"Gotta whiz?"

"No. Breakfast run."

"Make mine the usual."

He buttoned and zipped.

"Be right back."

They kissed and he was gone.

His kiss woke her.

"So soon?" She moistened her lips. "Ugh. My mouth tastes like the battle of Verdun was fought in there."

He put three sacks on the table, carried the fourth to the door.

"For the next of kin next door," he said.

When he opened the door the sun, like a fool in love, rushed in.

Eight thirty.

She took her toilet kit into the bathroom.

He returned.

She said: "Where'd you find breakfast? Flagstaff?"

"The seven stop and gobbles near here are closed for vacation, or out of business. I damn near drove to Flagstaff before I found one open. Had a wait for the waitress to find me. Another wait for the order. I also filled with the octane my wheels love. I also dodged tourists who didn't know a one-way from a freeway."

He uncapped the coffee.

"I'm done in the head."

"I already drained my third leg."

A knock at the door.

"Hey, boss, do we have time for more than a sit-down?"

"Give baby sister a break, will ya?" Karen said.

"That's what I was doin'. And do again. If there's time."

"Make it quick."

"That's how she likes it."

"That's what she *says,* Arnie." Karen popped a styrofoam lid.

"What are ya sayin'?"

"I said it."

"I have to get back to Arnholt while the Mayor's still able to soil his diapers," Steve said.

On the expressway Steve squinted at traffic behind him.

Nothing suspicious.

Not yet.

TWENTY-NINE

KAREN DOZED UNTIL THEY LEFT ARIZONA and approached the Colorado state line. Ahead were the San Juan Mountains, and Durango.

"What's the plan, man?" She covered a belch.

"We should make Denver by dusk. Arnholt by dawn."

"Winter out there."

The freeway was freshly plowed. The early afternoon sky was cloudy.

"Looks like another storm," he said.

"Change of plans?"

"Until the weather breaks."

She thumbed over her shoulder. "They probably need breeding time."

Steve engaged the turn signal. The van followed at the Durango on ramp.

The clerk at the first motel they came to said: "Storm up there. In the San Juans. Might drop here. Or might not. Can't predict what the weather will do. Not even these weather experts with their forty-dollar haircuts and phony baloney smiles can make it accurate a hundred percent of the time. So take your chances. Or shack here for the next day or two. That's how long it takes for these storms to drop on us, or blow themselves out. Usually, that is."

"Coffee shop serve passable grub?" Steve tossed the credit card on the register.

"Passable? Yes. Something to write home about? Only if you don't have anything else to write home about. Blue plate's usually liver and onions left over from lunch. Or sweetbreads, whenever we get the bull to stand still. Sometimes it's pork du jour. Pork steak. Pork eyes. Pork loins. Or ham. Hocks. Steak. With or without eggs. Four decent sides with all-uh them,

Assorted dinner breads. Veggie du jour. today it's peas. Not the snapping bright green ones; the pale green mooshy ones. Salad which is mostly lettuce, with a carrot slice, tomato slice and watered down oil and vinegar. Soup? Navy bean that looks, tastes like Army mule bean but it's aw-right. There's also yesterday's broth with one or two lentils, looking like two eyes without a skull to place them in. Or a pork slice, reminding me of a disembodied tongue. There's also tongue, sliced so thin it almost disappears in the broth. Or mebbe there's an okra and roast beef sliver. Forgot what today's soup is. And finally . . ."

"Thank you, Lord," Babe said.

"Finally, there's desert and I can talk all the night long about desert."

"Please, don't," Karen said.

Steve and Arnie sat on the couch—the only furniture on that side of the desk.

"We got squares, for the squares," the elderly clerk said. "Pound cake. Brownies. Vanilla iced cream for the apple pie slivers; iced topping's extra. Different cake wedges. Got eternity covered, so to speak. Devil's food and Angel food. Cake. All home made. By my missus."

Cued, a bloated, toothless, shaggy haired woman of late middle age appeared in an adjoining doorway. The one piece house dress was grease spotted, matching the lesions on her forehead. She wore frayed slippers and wool sox, gray as her complexion. The footwear did little to warm her swollen ankles and toes.

"She does the cooking?" Babe said.

"Every thing, honey," she said. "Party of four?"

"Uh, well." Babe looked at her husband.

"Yeah." He got to his feet.

"Uh, what he means is: no. Family meeting, family. Thanks for the chin music, mister."

"Thanks ain't necessary."

"I can be talked into visiting you boys," the woman said. "He won't mind. Will ya, Larkin?"

"Naw. Long's they treat ya like you're halfway human."

"We got all the company we can handle," Babe said. "What you can see." She touched her stomach. "Mebbe what you can't."

"Really?" they said.

"Riley. A family name and a good one for the first one that comes outta me. If there's anything in there that needs to be out here."

"Well, Hon, you look like you're carryin' precious cargo. I bore him an even foursome."

"It wasn't boring, I can tell ya. Walkin' softly until the deluge. Flooded four mattresses. Didn't ya, Opal?"

"That ain't something a lady brags about but, yeah, since you brought it up."

"Show them our quartet of little kickers."

"Naw, they ain't interested. Neither am I."

Karen and Steve linked arms. "Don't get too many folks to talk with, do ya, folks?"

"We talk a lot." She wiped saliva from sagging lips.

"All the time," Larkin said.

"Have a nice chat, you two," Karen said.

Outside, Babe said: "Before we do anything we better inspect the rooms."

The women went in. The men went to the van.

"Smell anything?" Arnie unlocked the doors.

"The old broad." Steve took the passenger's seat.

Arnie slid in on the driver's side.

"Smells like a snow storm."

The clerk came over. He wore a greatcoat, muffler, gloves. He shivered.

"Mister Jones. There's a problem with your credit card."

Arnie fell in beside Steve.

"What's the problem, boss?"

In the office, Steve said: "What's the problem?"

The clerk dropped the blinds over the front and side windows.

"No problem." From under the greatcoat he produced a sawed-off.

His wife cane out of the room behind the front desk. She

locked the door.

"Our business is with Mister Jones," she told Arnie.

"See ya?" Arnie said.

"Not just yet." Larkin gestured with the sawed-off.

Arnie crossed the shoe-box-shaped lobby, to the front desk.

"Show us what you got, boys." Opal wore dentures, deodorant and a sweater and skirt.

Arnie and Steve emptied their pockets on the counter. Larkin plucked the truck keys from the piled pocket debris.

Two men, carrying Russian AKs, came out of the adjoining room.

The taller of the two turned off the vacancy sign. Money changed hands.

Larkin and Opal went into the back room and shut the door.

The short gunman forced a friendly tone. "We're easy, Jones. When we're gone we won't return."

His partner compared the credit card photo with the trucker. Jones leaned against the counter.

"I know the economy is shit but why work this?"

"It isn't work. It's pleasure," one said.

"Worked for you, Jones," the other said.

The old couple left the room. Carried suitcases. She dropped keys on the counter.

"Be sure you give these to the Slayboughs. They have a set but in case they don't trust us, they'll have our set."

The tall man took the keys. "Why wouldn't they trust us?"

The ones not laughing were Jones and Barnes.

"We finished here?" Larkin said.

"The crew's right outside."

"We will wave when we leave." Larkin unlocked the door.

"Be sure you do."

"They'd be so hurt if you didn't."

More guffaws.

Through the open door the wind ruffled the register.

The old couple turned up their collars, holstered their weapons, rebuttoned their coats.

"Till next time, guys."

They hurried across the lot to their Cadillac.

Across the lot two men unlocked doors. Two men holding sawed-offs stood watch.

Babe and Karen were dragged out of their rooms. They were dressed, bleary eyed.

"The ladies are insurance," the tall man said.

"We'll drop them close by with enough quarters for the pay phone."

"Hijackers with manners," Steve said. "Who's paying you?"

"How deep is the ocean?"

"How high is the sky?"

The women were prodded to the office door.

"Helluva vacation," Babe said.

The taller of the two tossed the rig's keys to one of the crew. "Okay, ladies."

They were herded into the truck, onto the jump seat.

One went for chairs. The other watched the. prisoners.

A cockroach scurried across the watcher's shoe.

He yiped.

Arnie lunged.

The watcher danced away from the roach.

Arnie used his elbows and knees.

He and the gunman went down.

The chair-carrying hood's Russian AK was strapped across his chest. He dropped the chairs. Struggled to unholster the weapon.

Steve slammed into him.

He slammed his fist into the hood's groin.

"Yeeee!" The hood slammed into the desk, fell forward, into Steve's cocked elbow. The tall hood threw Steve off balance. He dropped onto his tail bone. The lower discs, if they could shout, would have awakened the dead in the morgue ten miles away.

Stunned, the trucker gagged.

The hood reached for the AK-47.

Arnie fired once.

The gunman flew back, collided with the desk. The register and pocket debris rained down.

Arnie swung, aimed at the short man's chest.

The sawed-off hood, propped against the wall, retched, spat, sneezed.

Steve moved. Jackhammered pain attacked his spine.

"How's the view down there, boss?"

"Wonderful." Steve fingered his ears until the ringing stopped.

"Do I drag short-cakes into the cold?"

"Let me tell you this. We weren't supposed to do this."

"Speak up. For the hearing impaired."

"Hold you here while the crew jacked the cargo, dropped the truck and the tramps."

"Tramps!" Arnie raised the rifle butt.

The hood lunged. Arnie side-danced. He struck the hood's shoulder.

Groaning, the hood rolled on the floor; his face white as death is dark.

"Lemme send him home, boss."

"We might need him. For bargaining. If he belongs to one of those butch thugs."

"Insulting people? That's what you're taught in truck driver's ed?"

Arnie slammed the butt into the man's thigh.

His voice skittered like a third rate horror flick sound effect.

Arnie said: "I didn't hear you say nothin' about makin' him behave."

"Don't need his no-tell intel."

"Know the answers, Jones? Getting old, Jones. A part-time jacker's got to know more intel than a pro who's out there, working, all the time." He smirked. "I'd make peace with the man, waiting for your ass."

"Highways are littered with mouths like yours."

"What's next?" Arnie said.

"Wait."

Arnie passed the AK to Jones. "Miss me when I'm gone?"

After the front door closed, the hood focused on his partner's diamond pinky ring.

"When you were away from your rig I installed the tracker. Larkin and Opal were back up. The Slayboughs went to Holly

Springs, Mississippi to visit their children. I created the plan. Now I share space with super-sized roaches."

"Your plan has more holes than a procto clinic."

Arnie parked the van by the door. He came in, Arms loaded.

"In case we meet the company." He checked the first weapon.

Doing seventy miles an hour, a van rolled in, skidded next to Arnie's four-wheel drive. Four jackers bailed, side arms drawn.

Arnie threw the hood against the wall. Plaster showered. Arnie used the gun butt. The scalp gash turned the gunman's coat collar darker.

"Call me if ya need me." Arnie hopped the counter, limped into the back room.

The crew leader pounded the counter.

"Where's the shit!"

His eyes were red as his cheeks. His lips tightened. His chin quivered. His hands trembled.

The three, lined up at the door, held shotguns. He brandished a three-fifty-seven.

"Where the fuck is it!"

"Right here." Arnie fired from the doorway.

The four scrambled for cover.

His mouth opened to spare his hearing, Jones squeezed a round.

Two squirmed on the floor, their weapons still firing, shredding the worn carpet, chipping cement.

The other two, at the door, squeezed rounds.

Ducking, firing, Arnie and Steve threw themselves in directions where the slugs weren't.

The smeared door front cracked. The reverb killed their squeaks.

Steve stepped around the carnage.

Outside, Arnie sucked in cold air.

"Makes a fool out of a good meal," Steve said.

"Sure does." Arnie went to the crew's van. "Someone ain't here. Shit! A pair of someones."

THIRTY

THEY FOUND THEM a mile down the road, behind the counter of a stop-n-shop store.

Their argument played out in harsh stage whispers while two customers waited.

Babe stocked the cigarette rack. Karen rang up a credit card purchase. The customer took his gallon of skim milk out the door, bumping into Steve and Arnie as they hurried in. Arnie's eyes and smile widened.

"Hello, boys." Karen put a lid on a styrofoam of coffee.

The customer paid and left.

"What's this?" Steve said at the counter.

"We had to do something," Karen said. "Waiting to be rescued."

"With the economy giving us the old ho-hum, we took what we could get." Babe came out from behind the counter. "Like I did once and never regretted it."

And into her husband's arms. "Hi-ya, handsome." She did a belly bump, and shared a long kiss.

"Why didn't you call?" Steve said between kisses.

"When we signed on, this joint was wall-to-wall customers. Who had time to call?"

"I never saw so many chumps buying six-packs, popcorn snacks, Ramble House paperbacks, racing magazines right off the racks," Babe said.

"The owner was busier than a one-legged roofing contractor at a ladder climbing contest."

"He'd been on his balls. Balls of his feet. For like fifteen hours," Babe said. "His relief clerk didn't show because of her monthly friend. He was stuck here for the duration."

"First thing he asked, in that cute sing-songy way they have, if we knew how these places worked."

"How to pump a cash register."

"Operate the gas pumps by remote."

"Stock shelves."

"And didn't mind doing a twelve hour day."

"For minimum wage."

"Since his was the only job offer of the day we accepted."

"And here we are. Wondering how you are."

After the up-date, Babe said: "When those guys saw what wasn't in the truck, they jumped around like their pricks were on fire."

"When did you re-plot the plants?" Karen said.

"No plot," Steve said.

"Like the last book I read," Karen said.

"When I went for breakfast in Kingman, I detoured, found a cold storage drop. That's where the stuff is. Why the bacon and eggs run took so long."

"They were so pissed they deserted the truck. In the middle of the freeway." Babe pointed. "I can damn near see it from here."

"Four more hours on the clock," Karen said.

"Have fun," Steve said.

"Me and the boss could use some zee-time, ladies." Arnie nodded at the door behind the counter.

"No cots, hot rocks," babe said. "A clean floor is all."

"Save some space for me," Steve, said, out the door.

The wind cut like a shank in a street fight. The street lights were like an old man's memory.

"Old man midnight," Steve said to himself. "Like a dead star."

It was a long two blocks to the expressway.

The rig abutted a cement island, blocking one lane.

One hinge held the rear door. The other hinge dangled.

Traffic inched past. No highway bulls in sight.

The motor rumbled like it was glad to see him, feel his hand unleashing the passion.

Margo had responded like that.

He released the hand brake. Shifted gears.

Cursed his father.

Not too late to do what had to be done.

He backed into the slot under the convenience store sentry light. He measured each step to the entrance.

"That didn't take long." Karen went to greet him.

Babe was in back behind the closed door.

An old man in a frayed jacket and creaseless work pants waited for the chili dog to warm.

"Kid," Steve nuzzled her hair, "you smell sweeter than mother's milk."

"Mother's milk has a warm, sugary taste. The customers don't mind it, but what do they know?"

She pressed an ear to his chest.

"Still beating?"

"Do you wear a pacemaker?"

"Microwave."

"Supper time." Cackling, the old man reached. Quivering fingers guided the twelve incher to trembling lips. He groaned, gummed, belched, farted, stuffed the last of it, wiped his nose and mouth on his sleeve.

"Now if I only had a cold drink to wash it down."

Karen pointed to the sign next to the cooler.

"Aw, shuckens." He looked at his curled shoe tops. "I paid the last of the loot for that treat that's makin' me toot."

"Sorry, bo," she said. "This ain't a y'all-come homeless flop."

"Well, how 'bout lettin' me do the do? Ya know. Use the comforts."

"Do what you always do," Steve said.

Those old eyelids tightened.

"And what would that be?" His voice dropped. He reached into the jacket pocket.

"Shit in the bushes. Don't mean the George Bushes."

Steve's fists remained at his side.

"That's what they're for. Isn't that what you ball-footers do?"

The trembling fingers remained in the pocket. "I ain't a ball, whatever you said."

"Don't you walk on the balls of your feet? Come up behind folks with a shank and attitude?"

"All I got's the need to be freed." He waved a box cutter. "Git outta my passway."

Steve stepped aside. "Door's right over there, bo."

"I'm broke. Not blind."

Eyes trained on the trucker, he side-shuffled out the door. Steve followed. The bum eyeballed the rig.

"Keep moving, Rockefeller."

The old man flashed the finger. Steve stepped out of the doorway light.

"Jus' kiddin'."

The tramp trotted on arthritic knees and ankles into the darkness that crouched beyond the sentry light.

"Another great adventure," Karen said when Steve came back in.

"I have no sympathy for them. My truck's been vandalized more than once. After a while the claims people accused me of working a con. That's when I went into business with your folks. Then with Lance."

"Nobody meddled Tilly and Bert."

"Nobody diddled Harry Lance till now."

He yawned, stretched. His discs popped. He clenched his jaw to keep from screaming.

"Need a lie down?"

"Four hours before you're off the clock?"

"Closer to three."

"I'm out in the truck."

Midnight.

Karen tapped on the driver's door.

Steve rolled the window.

She showed a fat envelope.

"Close to a hundred in smalls for me and mine."

Babe and her bounce came over.

"Should've seen the guy cry when they gave notice," Arnie said.

Karen gave Steve a styrofoam.

"Hope you like strong coffee."

"A strong woman." He pointed.

Arnie was at the window.

"What about your credit card, boss?"

On the road, Karen said: "Get some sleep?"

"Not much."

"When we get home."

"That's when the work starts."

The highway bulls, police and sheriff and her deputies huddled in the motel lobby.

Steve's credit card topped a pile on the counter.

The armor, piled in a corner, was being inventoried by four ATF agents. Shell casings under foot, kicked away with a curse.

The other debris was gone. Their blood soaked the carpet, stained the cement under it, brought out the roaches.

The sewer hit them whenever an agent or deputy carried out the weapons.

The wind couldn't flush the victims final act.

"Guess we gotta do our dance." Babe got out.

They went under the tape and went in. A deputy stopped them.

"Crime scene. Like the tape says."

"It didn't speak to us." Babe played innocent the way Perlman played Mozart.

"Our men. Oh, I wonder." Karen's hand flew to her mouth. "Was it them? I hope not."

"Tell us," the sheriff said from the couch across the room.

"We met the boys in the coffee shop over there. They paid for the meal. Seemed nice. What happened?" Babe wiped a tear, swallowed a sob.

"Did you get their names?"

"Pete was one."

"Thomas was mine."

"He was mine. Yours was Pete."

"Now, hon, you got it wrong."

"Ladies, ladies, save the wrestle," the sheriff said. "Let's see some ID"

They showed 1099s from the stop-n-shop.

"I recognize Hakim's scrawl," the sheriff said. "He issues withholding forms every shift."

"If the stop-n-shop can't keep employees, who will the perps shoot at?"

"Folks, we've been on our feet twelve hours," Karen said. "Our arches and piles hate us."

"What else do you know?" an officer said.

"Nothing else."

"Wait now, sister." Babe dropped a hand on Karen's arm. "Mine's name was Thomas. He said he and Pete had some kind of quick job that'd pay well. We had to get to our jobs so we let them pay our check."

"Is there a delayed echo in the room?" the sheriff said. "Because we just heard that."

"Yes, ma'am," Karen said. "But you didn't hear us tell you this."

"Cuz we haven't said it yet."

"They promised to pick us up after our shift."

"All they're going to pick up now is basic technique." The sheriff scratched a cheek mole. "How to decompose in the bone yard."

Babe and Karen yawned in the sheriff's face.

The sheriff waved a hand. "Stale coffee and dental caries."

"That shit does carry."

"Nobody's perfect."

"My Tommy said I was close to perfect." Babe executed an eye-take.

"Tommy was mine, stupid." Karen inched toward the desk. "Yours was Pete."

"Yeah?" Babe showed her fists. "Who sez?"

"I sez, dim bulb." Karen dropped a hand on the pile.

"Yeah?"

"Yeah!"

"Shit. I got the flashes and these dumb daisies are doing a dance."

The sheriff wiped her pocked forehead.

"A lotta Ds there, sheriff," Babe said.

"Show them what the door is for. Somebody."

"We know where it is." Babe started for it, stumbled on shell casings. Steadied herself.

In the few seconds it took to keep from falling, Karen palmed the card.

"It's that oblong of cracked glass and red smears." Karen followed her out.

Someone said: "Looks like an arms deal gone to crap."

"Durango doesn't have that sort of crime."

"It does now."

The door swung shut behind them.

The sheriff came out.

"Where's the credit card?"

She said it like Burger King's Clara Pealer would say it.

"Don't know nothing about credit cards," Babe said.

"We are strictly debit darlings."

They kept walking.

THIRTY-ONE

ARNIE AND STEVE WERE AROUND THE CORNER in a multi-plex lot.

The theaters were closed. Four sentry lights burned.

His foot on the van's running board, Arnie retied his boot.

Steve double checked the rig's cargo doors.

In the van, Babe slept.

In the truck, Karen was awake.

"I have to get this said, Steve. I don't know how to say it."

"I understand English."

"We can't go back and fix things."

"Back where?"

"The ditch. Where Gray and his van did their last rites. Couple things happened."

"Like the flying elephant said: 'I'm all ears'."

"I'm all fears. About your reaction. Arnie's, too."

The truck ahead slowed for the turn. Steve geared down.

"Just say it."

A pause. Then:

"The few times we were together I never had the courage to tell you what I need sometimes. When I need it the juice flows like the Red Sea over Pharaoh's army. Nick Gray also had a need. To humiliate. He also had a tiny tackle box. A box full of the stuff that dreams are made of. Baby making dreams. What he did to me was a win-win. For him and me."

"Okay."

He used the turn signal.

They were on the Durango exit ramp.

"When Nick got me naked and down, the bitch sheriff and her dancin' daughter bitch held me down in the mud. They jerked my hips up, held 'em up, spread my butt cheeks. I knew before his cock kissed my ass crease what was gonna happen. The traditional prison hello. They laughed when he pumped his shaft. Then he jammed it in, filled my hole with his pain maker. He went in deep. No lube. No slow and easy in. No "sorry" when I screamed. The broads shrieked. He started shooting. The hot cum scalded, tickled, teased, started my bowels surging. I gagged. Belched. Farted. I threw my hips side to side, up and down like I was on loco weed. They let me go. He pinned me, thrashed me, cursed me. I held it until he pulled out, spilling his spum on my heaving asscheeks. He rubbed the jizz all over my fat ass. He grunted, breathed hard. I felt it on my lower back. I was afraid he was gonna do it again right then. Like most men he was done for the duration. At least with me. Sobbing with pain and rage, I squatted and not even paying attention to the bitches' taunts, I did me a shit like I haven't done in a while. His fuck-enema gave me the best shit I could've hoped for. Meantime, Nick was busting Babe. They held her down. He fucked her in the missionary way. It was easy-rape. She spilled sex juice when his cock thickened. Like me, she likes it differently every so often. It balances the loving moves that Arnie makes. Like with me, it was a quick cum and a fast go. What Arnie knows about Babe and you don't. She's been ovulating like crazy. Like those eggs gotta drop or she will."

She daubed her eyes.

"I'm scared when it comes down the eerie canal and looks anything like Nick Gray, well, I'd hate to see Arnie hurt and Babe dead. Because sure as guard dogs bark and farts stink, if she drops Gray's whelp, Arnie will kill her."

She glanced at Steve's profile.

"When you and Arnie came into the store, she and me were arguing about letting it happen, and praying every day and twice at night. Or ending it."

"She wants it?"

She nodded.

"Any suggestions?"

"Hope for a miscarriage."

Four A. M.

Traffic flowed on the interstate northeast toward Denver and Aurora.

"Ortha used to butt fuck me. Made me jump and shout."

He squinted at approaching high beams.

He said: "Hand me those shades. In the glove compartment."

She did.

"While little meat was thrumming it into me, tearing me up in there, I wanted to kill him. Or be killed."

"Glad it didn't. I hate graveyards."

They hit pot-holes. He activated the wipers. Slush evaporated from the windshield.

"When do we eat?"

"There's a diner between Aurora and Denver. Good eats. Clean crappers."

"Do they sell things?"

"Such as?"

"All my stuff's at the motel."

"Nothing with your name on it?"

"DNA maybe. They have to catch me first."

"They sell toothpaste. Lottery Tickets. Cells. The usual."

Slush hit the front window. Where the wipers didn't reach, the gouts slid like passing years in prison.

She watched, wondered, worried.

"The cargo."

"What about it?"

"Are you selling it?"

"Not right away. I want it close. Kingman's temporary. Until I find another space." He glanced. "I could dump the load in your yard but why trouble you?"

"Russian Thistles love company."

"When I move it maybe you'll help."

"I dunno about me. Heavy lifting's strenuous for a broad like me."

"A broad like you could lead an army into battle."

"Let's hope I don't have to."

"I heard that." She belched.

"Heard that, too."

"Not the first time."

"A belching, farting woman with blood in her. Helluva combo."

"Don't know about the blood. While he was in me, I thought about you."

"Don't know how to answer that."

"Don't have to."

When they passed Aurora, and were within yelling distance of Denver it was seven thirty.

"We are close, hon."

"Oh." She rubbed sleep crusts, stretched as best she could in the cramped cab. "Man, I gotta squat."

"Can you wait for indoor plumbing?"

"Have to."

Off the interstate, south to the few houses, farm land, and one diner.

The neon above the bungalow-styled eatery read: "Eppworth Webbler. Our Specialty."

"What do you suppose that is?" she said.

"Owners' names. The dish is Shepherd's Pie without the 'baaahhhh'."

They waited by the door for Babe and Arnie.

They asked for family seating.

The one booth, by the window, was syrup and coffee spotted.

Half full cups and almost empty plates littered the Formica.

The waitress shut the blinds.

Sun slivers radiated off the car hoods, came through the blinds' slits.

They waited by the booth while the soiled dishes were bused, the table damp-ragged, the linoleum under the booth swept.

"What's this Eppworth Webbler?" Babe said.

The waitress pitched it, eyeing them, figuring if they were tippers or all night tipplers.

"It looks like a giant pot pie. Chopped steak or turkey, potato buds, veggies in a cream sauce, all wrapped in a flaky browned crust. Comes with hash browns, juice and coffee or hot tea."

After they ordered, Karen went to the notions counter in back, bought what she needed. Covering her mouth, she rushed into the bathroom.

"Big sis lookin' pretty gray in the gills," Arnie said.

"I better go see."

Babe slid out of the booth.

"Sweetest ass in this part of the world." Arnie winked.

"Older sis isn't?"

"Boss, if Babe wasn't available I'd give Karen the hot eye."

"She'd give it right back."

"Hey, good words from across the table."

A coffee carafe and hot water pot arrived. Two tea bags in paper sleeves fell from the waitress's hand. She leaned the bags against the water pot.

"Need refills on anything, my name's Johnnie Mae." After a sip of the strong, black sludge, Steve said: "Karen told me about the rape."

Arnie's hand tightened around the cup.

"She told me who did it." Arnie's eyes were vacant.

"What else?"

"She told me Karen was raped prison style. I hope she didn't get anything worse than piles."

"Arnie, what worries Karen is how you feel about it."

"Pissed off. Glad that I sent him away."

"With him gone, who's left?"

Arnie thought before he said: "You're right. There's Harry, who ain't worth the trouble."

Jones emptied two sugar packs.

"Like I already said, boss, me and she are trying to make it a threesome. She told me about him being an ass banger; Karen might see a doctor for damage, and worse. He also screwed Babe without a condom. First worry was AIDS. He was a big, healthy dude so he might not have it. The second worry is her getting pee-gee by the wrong dickster. I'd like the little squealer to look like its ma, not this beat down ex-man of the streets. Hell, if my nose was any flatter it'd be coming out my ear. "If what she has in her tank looks like Prince Little Meat who ain't with us anymore, that'd be oh-jay-jake by me. It's what the kid grows up to be." He took a sip. "Who he looks like don't matter a whole lotta rat holes. Coffee tastes fresh."

The bathroom door opened.

The girls came out.

Babe was all smiles.

Karen looked stunned.

"Guess what, guys," Babe said. "We are pregnant."

THIRTY-TWO

AT NINE THIRTY THEY PASSED FORT MORGAN.

McCook, across the Colorado-Nebraska border, was the town they would pass before they reached Freemantle.

Steve said: "When?"

Karen said: "Remember that roll on the rug two months back?"

"Not much happened, cum-wise."

"Doesn't take much. Hell, daddy, I'm not only big, I'm healthy. And fertile."

"There's a new doctor at the McCook clinic. Doctor Okosi. She specializes in pre-natal care."

"How do you know this?"

"She sees most anyone. I saw her awhile back for my back. She told me what her specialty was."

"At my age. Can't believe it."

"Doin what I did's some kind of sign."

"Not only what *you* did. I didn't just lay there with my flat feet pointed at Heaven."

"I suppose you want a church wedding."

"Says who?"

"I just did."

"What about what I want?"

"Isn't that what you want?"

"I'd really like old man Johnson to know what he won't ever see."

"If he paid his debts with cow droppings he still wouldn't give a cow turd to see his grandchild."

He eased into the turning lane.

"Are you still worried about Babe?"

"Look what she night drop. I got the pick of the litter, the best of the breed."

On the far side of the "Welcome To McCook" sign one man paced.

He wore a greatcoat, boots, gloves, ear muffs, a muffler and fur-lined cap.

He wore a sandwich sign: "Don't be a dummy. Use a condom in her cunny."

"Now he tells me," they said. They exchanged looks.

"I didn't mean it, Steve. It must be the hormones."

"I worry about my checking account after I pay off the family. Pay for the back surgery."

"Oh? That's news."

"Not to me. There's the cut doctoring. The post op. The rig goes into storage for the duration."

He slowed, gave an arm signal.

Arnie drove alongside.

"Got to make another stop, kid."

"I'll follow you, pops."

Steve forced the smile.

THIRTY-THREE

AFTER THE EXAM Karen was escorted to the reception area.

The crew searched for cold storage.

McCook had the nearby Daub Industrial Park which abutted the Fahey Landfill. Twenty-four hour secure storage was the guarantee.

After reserving a storage bay they picked up Karen.

"How'd it go?" Steve folded the reservation slip.

"Feet in the stirrups. Like I was mounting *Who Doctor Who* for a run for the roses. Doc Okosi reminded me I was the one who got mounted and we had a sisterly chuckle about that."

Her eyes were luminous.

Tears moistened the lashes.

Ridges bracketed her mouth.

Her full lips flattened against her teeth.

"Steve, you do want this?"

"I will. After I finish with Johnson."

"As far as marriage goes, let it go."

"I hope to be around for the first birthday."

"Longer?"

"Yes."

Borne along by a listless breeze, snow, light as ash, swept across the snub-nosed hood, gathered against the windshield's bottom frame.

Outside Freemantle Arnie used the horn, cut in front of the rig, and, staying at the fifty-five MPH maximum, out-distanced the truck by a half mile.

"He can't wait to get in her bloomers," Karen said.

"Were you ever that young, Steve?"

"Half hard. Always."

"Even with the back problem?"

"No problem back then. Decades of coffee, not milk, made the problem."

He clenched the wheel.

"Bad?"

"Been worse."

"If there was something I could do, I'd do it."

"Take care of yourself."

"You do the same."

"Sounds like, well, what it sounds like."

"Like two lovers about to have the last kiss before the train pulls out," she said. "With fog, tears and close ups. And coat lapels buttoned, hems flapping against knees as the lovers hurry across the platform. What movie was that from?"

"It was . . . I think it was from the cable version of that novel: *Strangers At The Dance*." A lifting, dropping of his bony shoulders. "Or not."

Thick fog plummeted. Freemantle's western edge faded. Steve used the highway lights.

Freemantle's post office and bank were side by side.

The postmaster and bank president's two-story, colonaded homes shared a lot line.

The twin street lights went on.

"Lights of home," she said.

The overhead traffic signal, locked in the yellow setting, was fog-smeared.

He cut the wheel. Turned onto the winding four-laner. Up the incline. To the house a quarter mile beyond.

Their driveway curved past the house and dead-ended at the four-car garage by the rear privacy fence.

"Mind if I store the rig?"

"Store away."

When he entered the kitchen, she tossed the van's keys.

"Coffee?"

"A piss and I'm gone."

He dropped the truck's keys on the counter.

She picked them up.

"Hurry back."

"I hope."

THIRTY-FOUR

TWO ROBINS FLEW LOW toward alley scraps. Their shadows flickered across Arnholt's chipped, muddy curbs. The fog lifted to the tree tops. The sun was a sluggish reminder of late Autumn.

Four P.M.

The line that began at one end of the block and ended at the diner didn't react to the van or its driver.

The walking dead, one at a time, shuffled into the diner. After receiving the weekly subsistence check, each recipient shambled out the rear exit.

Two John Wayne-sized uniformed men handled crowd control. They carried police specials on their hips.

Recon complete, Steve U-turned and drove west one mile to Grace Smith's house. It was dark. Editions of Omaha's daily paper were piled against the front door.

No sign of life in there.

He tried front and back doors. Locked tighter than a miser's cash box.

He limped to the van.

The wind formed snow humps against the front tires.

Groaning, he broke two calcium tabs from the blister pack.

A pickup slid, slowed, stopped alongside the van.

"Figured you might try what that big ass bigot who wrote those shitty novels said you can't ever do," Arnie said.

"Who?"

"That hillbilly who scribbled those books that were bigger than a hooker's pussy. Forced to read them's the reason I quit school."

"Don't know . . ."

"What he said was: you can't go home again."

"Mona hasn't. Bring friends?"

"Spread out. Easy reach. How much muscle?"

"Two at the diner. That's all I saw. Thirty-eights in plain sight."

"Forty-sevens trump thirty-eights." Arnie got in. "Now or later?"

"Now."

THIRTY-FIVE

THE LINE OUTSIDE THE DINER WAS GONE.

They were a half block away and across the street.

The two guards, at the counter, sipped tea.

Arnie said: "Don't see the old man."

"Taking a late afternoon sit-down." Steve went in.

Vicki, behind the counter, saw him, grinned.

He opened his coat. When she saw what he reached for she backed behind the pots and pans rack.

The guards turned their heads.

Jones AK was aimed at the space between the pair.

"Where's the old dog?"

"Behind you."

Mayor Johnson stood in the rear doorway. He held a sawed-off.

Arnie came in. The Russian AK was aimed high enough to take off the old man's head.

"Ain't this cozy." Arnie was close enough for the kill, far enough to avoid the splatter.

"Kinda reminds me of that painting of a diner and the coffee sippers."

Vicki came out of the kitchen. She pointed a sawed-off at Steve, then at Johnson.

The guards looked at each other.

"Who do I kiss? The dude who walked away with my cherry or the dude who keeps the lights burning?"

She aimed at Steve's forehead.

Sidearms drawn, the John Waynes faced Arnie.

The gunman held steady. He didn't blink.

Johnson said: "Helluva hello for your father."

Keeping Jones in muzzle-sight, the old man moved into the room.

"Before we start spilling." Jones sat at the counter, eleven feet from the mayor. "I have what you want, Mister I-will-rule-the-world. You may find it. You may die first. Or you may go nuts, looking."

"Or, you will give it up right now."

"If you think I will, you're not thinking."

Johnson closed in. "Finish your tea, boys."

"I can't miss, boss."

"Stand down, Arnie."

Arnie backed toward the front door. He held the AK chest high.

One of the guards faced Arnie. The other moved in on Steve.

Johnson pulled a chair into the aisle between tables. His ass came down on the hard wood like a boulder falling in slow motion.

One elbow rested on the plastic-littered table top. The others tucked at his side, braced the sawed-off.

"Sit, boy. Negotiate."

"Without the audience." Seated at the counter, Steve slumped. His back faced Vicky.

"The audience stays."

"Watch your mail." Steve pushed off the stool. His hand braced against the counter. His spine cracked. He bumped the counter.

He gripped the clammy edge.

The John Waynes moved closer.

"Don't need an escort." Steve rubbed his eyes.

"May I interest you in pallbearers?"

Johnson's dead eyes. Like muddy lumps.

"What do you need to get you out of here and out of my life, son?"

Silence.

Then; their labored breathing. A faucet's dripping. The wind brushing the front window, rattling the glass, making the steel frame sing.

"Say it before I get much older."

"I have it."

"I will find it."

"Start looking."

"An interesting challenge. Right, boys?"

They nodded.

"I'm feeling generous, Steve. After all, you are my only child. I will buy the cargo. Name the price?"

"Not for sale, daddy."

Johnson sighed, said: "You certainly are your mother's child. All right. What are the terms?"

"Let me enjoy your frustration a while longer."

Johnson shrugged. "Waiting is my long suit."

"Doesn't it piss you off that you lost the money and the boodle?"

"A day in the life."

The wind dropped.

The door shook.

Arnie dropped the deadbolt.

A finger tapped the sweating glass.

"Chase your tail." Arnie's voice echoed in the high-ceilinged room.

"Read any books lately? Only in fiction do the bad guys get screwed, and good triumphs."

"Hey!" The voice penetrated the double-paned glass. "Out of food? Or what?"

"Private party!" Arnie said.

"All we want's coffee!"

"Cream and sugar!"

"Two cheeseburgers!"

"With the works!"

"Extra large portion of those vein-busting fries!"

Arnie said: "Don't you guys pick up what's bein' put down?"

"We don't have to!"

"We're the highway patrol!"

Arnie shoved the Russian AK under his greatcoat. He moved away from the door.

"Crap!" Vicki waddled to the door. "I got to do everything."
She unbolted the lock.

Two highway bulls came in, with a wind burst that made her nipples throb.

The bull said: "Any trouble, Mayor?"

"Might say so." Johnson nodded at Jones and Arnie.

The officers pulled their pieces.

"Rank trumps armor, son. I have both."

"Not quite, honey." Vicki pulled the trigger.

Johnson's face swelled with rage and fear. His forehead and cheeks blushed before his face disappeared. The blast's force threw him out of the chair. He and the chair slammed the wall. The liquids lubed his slide to the floor.

A sleeve brushed the space heater. The singed flannel gave off a soap and fabric softener odor.

No one moved or spoke.

When hearing returned, the bull said: "There goes the dinner break."

"There goes my appetite." His partner holstered his sidearm.

"Get going," one of the troopers said.

The John Waynes grabbed their jackets from the rack by the entrance.

"Not too far, fellas."

The JWs slipped on the sidewalk, skirted the snow banks and ice islands along the building's west edge.

"There goes no help, " Arnie said.

"Why, sis?" the troopers said.

"He was filth." Her eyes brimmed with hate. "Forced me to do filth. Stopped paying for the filth. Tired of being short changed. Hell, no changed. Tired of cooking meals he bitched about and never paid for. Tired of him stinking up the place. Dammit, Wendell, I'm trapped in this graveyard, thanks to him. Well, shit, I'm trapped no more."

The troopers began to speak.

She rushed on.

"He rapped about how worthless I was, how I'd never be loved. A smart man, or a considerate one, would never tell that to a woman. But I believed him. Played my hurdy gurdy with no hope of ever getting a real man on me, in me. Then big stud on wheels over here—the Jones with the bones—came in and hurt me so badly I had to free myself. So I just did. My two choices. Swallow the muzzle. Or use it for good. I think I did a hundred or so bodies some good with a single shot. Might even erect a statue in my honor."

"Vic, you won't be here to see it."

"Drive you to Omaha."

"Put you on a one-way outta here."

"Got your passport?"

"Pissport," she said. "Never used it."

"Use it now!"

"Canada's no worse than Nebraska in winter."

"We'll sell this place."

"Send you the money."

She kissed them.

"Thanks, guys."

"Well, hurdy gurdy," Steve said.

Her lips flattened cheek stubble.

"Someone needs a shave."

"Everyone' s a critic." Steve returned it.

"Nothin' for me?" Arnie tilted his head.

"Before this turns into an orgy, Vic, you best pack."

"Get to Omaha before the weather gets worse."

Wendell said: "Sir, did you see what went on here?"

"You, getting kissed. Otherwise, I saw nothing."

"Helluva clean up." Vicki hip-switched to the hall, through the door and up the stairs to her crib.

"How're the roads?" Steve said, at the door.

"About what you'd expect after freezing drizzle."

"Not much snow."

They were outside.

"Be careful where you throw out your feet and you'll be awright," Wendell said.

Arms waving, Steve slipped, fell on his back with enough force to pop his lower plate.

THIRTY-SIX

JONES WAS MEDI-VACED TO MCCOOK.

Arnie drove down later that night.

During the drive he explained to Babe and Karen what had happened at the diner.

"Long dismal drive." Babe looked out the window.

"Nearest ER," Karen said.

They didn't discuss what had happened.

Dr. Okosi met them in the reception area.

"He mashed two discs. He's being prepped right now."

"Can we see him?" Karen said.

"He's under the sheet."

"Sheet?" they said.

"That's a cut doctor term. It means he's anesthetized."

The women grinned.

Arnie looked puzzled.

"Out here, Mr. Barnes, we have to reach for our humor."

"Don't let it bite ya on the ass."

"What I meant was . . ."

"He's knocked out."

"Better than being knocked up." Karen massaged her belly.

"Now, sister." Dr Okosi's tone was gentle.

Then she turned to Arnie.

"He's in deep sleep. Anesthetized."

"He don't have insurance so I figured you'd give him nothin' except the blade."

"We are government-funded."

"He'll get the best care, then."

"The very best. When he's in recovery I will let you know."

The ladies asked for directions to the bathroom.

Arnie said: "Where's the coffee shop?"

"Coffee pot's over there. Vending machines around the corner."

She was paged.

She went through double doors near the reception desk.

Arnie scratched, stretched. He glanced at the regional university's literary journal. It featured the abridged novel: *Strangers At The Dance.*

He yawned through the first chapter, tossed it on the magazine pile across from the low-slung table. He used the table for a footrest, and was dreaming about Babe when she slapped the bottom of his right foot.

"Huh?" He sat up, eyes darting.

"Wired as a wet noodle. Like always. What's the dream this time?"

He paused.

Then:

"We was on the highway. The trooper who pulled us over called it a ho-way, because the ho traffic from both coasts through Nebraska was heavy. He was their pimp. Offered me whatever I wanted. What I wanted, I told him, was what I already had, and she was no ho. She was you, hon. Better a hon than a ho."

"Why, Arnie Barnes. That's the sweetest mouthful you ever dumped in my lap."

"Speaking of dumping." Karen power-walked to the crapper.

"She sure was in a hurry," Arnie said. "Think it was my breath?"

"Possible. Pee gee broads get very sensitive, especially at first."

Arnie's belly growled. "Wonder what's for supper?"

A week later, Karen said: "'The slicer said the slice was successful."

She propped his pillow.

"Four months in a chair, then crutches, and P.T. for four more. Then the road."

"I passed the over the road test yesterday."

"Hey, great. But should you?"

"I'm knocked not teetering on the edge of a grave. Hooked up with a developer from Vancleave, Mississippi; he's dealing out of the diner. He's buying pieces of Arnholt at fair market, and, as an inducement, he's offering free furniture shipping anywhere in the country. He has loading and unloading crews. He also has a driver. Me. Eight months of steady work until our ten tons of fun comes out of the chute."

"Doin' aw-right so far?"

"So far it feels like a ton and three fourths in there. Another two tons and I'll piss a river. Only a gallon now. At night, mostly. After baby is off the tit I'm back working the wheel and you can be the stay at home. Work for you?"

"Has to."

Over the satellite music system:

"If the cops don't knock. If the pawnbrokers still hock." Karen sang:

"If we can walk a block. Raise your cock. Raise a flock. Of kids like us. Who eat and cuss. And make a fuss. About just us."

"Little late to worry about justice."

"Never too late."

"Keep reminding me."

"Who else do I have?"

"Who else do you need?"

The door opened.

"Room in here for us?" Arnie said.

"Come on In, kids." Karen's stomach rumbled. "Orders from headquarters."

She fled the room, for the uni-sex bathroom down the hall.

"Stevie, we brought your beverage." Babe set a styrofoam on the bedside table.

Arnie took the chair. "Say, have ya heard the one about the driver and the politician?"

"Let me tell it." She elbowed him off the chair.

Through the closed door laughter could be heard.

THE END

www.ingramcontent.com/pod-product-compliance
Lightning Source LLC
Chambersburg PA
CBHW030341030726
47499CB00003B/861